FATHER
TURIDDU
RETURNS:

A NOVEL

Daniel Conway

FATHER
TURIDDU
RETURNS:
THE CARDINAL AND THE INQUISITOR

A NOVEL

Riverwood Press
Louisville, KY

Front cover description

Napoli, an ancient city that many consider to be Italy's darkest, most dangerous and yet most fascinating place, is the setting for the encounter between Father T's friend The Cardinal and his mortal enemy, The Grand Inquisitor.

Back cover description

St. Peter's Basilica, one of the most famous churches in the world, viewed from the Via Conciliazione, Father T's temporary headquarters during his special assignment in Rome to save his friend the Cardinal from the terrorists' Grand Inquisitor.

Copyright © 2013 Daniel Conway

Published by: Riverwood Press Louisville, KY

ISBN 978-0615884936

Cover and interior design by Jane Lee
Sketches by Mark Castillo, Copy editing by William R. Bruns

Printed and bound in the United States of America

IN MEMORIAM
Msgr. William J. Lyons

BORN
September 5, 1930
Boston, Massachusetts

PRIESTHOOD ORDINATION
March 17, 1956
Archdiocese of St. Louis

DIED
November 21, 2011
Rome, Italy

Msgr. William J. Lyons, 81, a priest of the Archdiocese of St. Louis, who following many years of pastoral service in parishes, campus ministry and seminary education had served faithfully as a spiritual director for the North American College (NAC) since 2003, passed away on Monday November 21, 2011.

Msgr. Lyons was a classmate and friend of Msgr. Salvatore E. Polizzi, the inspiration for "Father Turiddu." Unlike the character in this novel, "Msgr. Leone," he did not retire and return to the United States but died in Rome while serving as a spiritual director at the NAC nearly a year before the events in this fictional narrative.

According to his wishes, Msgr. Lyons was interred in the Mausoleum of the Pontifical North American College in Campo Verano in Rome.

AUTHOR'S NOTE

This is a work of fiction. While it's true that certain characters have been inspired by real people (living and deceased), all of the situations, events and conversations contained in this story are the work of my imagination. Names have been changed (ever so slightly) to protect the innocent.

I wish to express my sincere gratitude to the real Cardinal who is the inspiration for my fictional character for taking the time to read my manuscript, make suggestions for improvement and bless this undertaking. I'm told by Msgr. Sal Polizzi (aka Father T) that the Cardinal called him when he was halfway through the manuscript and said, "Sal, How are we ever going to get out of that tower in Naples?"

"Father T and friends
rescue the Cardinal from
the clutches of the
Grand Inquisitor"

DAY ONE.
AFTERNOON.

Father T was in the kitchen of his rectory preparing spaghetti and meatballs for the ladies of the parish. Once a month he cooked for the ladies. "It's the least I can do," he always said. "Without their help, I couldn't keep this parish going."

St. Roch was a city parish. The past 30 years had seen a profound revitalization of the parish, school and its neighborhood from the days when the old archbishop told Father T to "save St. Roch" from the devastation caused by white flight and the resulting urban decay. Still, there was lots of work to do and many people to help.

Cooking for "the ladies" was Father T's way of showing his appreciation for the many contributions they made to people in the neighborhood—whether parishioners or not—who needed a helping hand. From the elderly shut-ins to families whose breadwinners were out of work, to people struggling with a loved one's cancer or a recent death in the family, The Ladies of St. Roch were a caring and consoling presence. They could also be a formidable force to be reckoned with whenever someone got in their way!

Monsignor Salvatore E. Turiddu, who everyone called Father T, knew how important the ladies were. He made sure that he thanked them often and, just as importantly, that he gave them a free hand in serving people's needs. "They know I'm the pastor of this parish," he said, "but they also know that I trust them to do whatever is necessary, and I'll support them no matter what."

Fr. T's spaghetti and meatballs were legendary. The meatballs were handmade and baked, not fried. And for the sauce, he used tomatoes from his own garden and seasonings that his mother and oldest sister taught him to mix-in following a recipe handed down from many generations of Sicilian families. The pasta was cooked al dente and removed from the boiling water at just exactly the right moment. When combined with his meatballs and sauce, everyone agreed, it was a meal "to die for."

As Father T stirred the huge pot containing his sauce, his cell phone began to vibrate in his shirt pocket. The caller ID told him it was Father Mike Belcamp, one of his closest friends and a frequent cooking and baking partner—especially during the holidays. Father Mike had served with Father T many years ago as an associate pastor. Now he worked for Catholic Cemeteries and was highly regarded by all who knew him.

"Hey, kid," Father T said. "I'm making my spaghetti and meatballs for the ladies. Come over for supper tonight and join me." (Father T served the ladies in the parish hall, but he didn't eat with them. Once he was sure that everyone had plenty to eat, he would prepare a plate for himself and take it back to the rectory kitchen.)

"I can't, Sal. I'm helping the Norcini brothers plan their big charity dinner next month. Why don't you join us for dinner at the Osteria after you've served the ladies?

We'll be finished with our meeting by then."

"Not tonight, Mike. I have a young man coming in for convert instructions at 7:30, and when we're finished I'm going to watch soccer on satellite TV. Italy is playing Brazil, and both teams are undefeated."

"Sal, the reason I called is because I heard something very strange this afternoon. A friend who works in the Vatican texted me that the Cardinal has been moved from his residence on the Via Conciliazione to a room inside the Vatican "for his protection.""

"Huh? Are you talking about our Cardinal? That's insanity."

"Yes," Father Mike said, "Our Cardinal. Evidently he has received several death threats, and the Vatican's security people are taking them very seriously."

"Who's behind these threats and why?" Father T asked with growing concern for the Cardinal, a man he deeply respected.

"My friend didn't know. He said the Vatican really wants to keep this quiet—especially from the media. The official story is that the Cardinal has gone away 'on holiday.' No one believes that, of course. The Synod of Bishops is only half finished. There's no way the Cardinal would take a vacation now."

Father T was stunned. He considered the Cardinal a close friend in spite of the fact that Father T was 20 years older and not an intellectual like his former archbishop, who was called to Rome to lead the Apostolic Signatura, the Church's Supreme Court.

When he was Father T's archbishop, the Cardinal was no stranger to controversy. While a gentle and gracious man personally, he was known to be an outspoken hardliner on matters of faith and morals. The local media had been merciless in its portrayal of him as a reactionary bishop with no understanding or compassion. They loved to bait him on social issues such as contraception, gay rights and the ordination of women, and they counted on his "no nonsense" responses which articulated the Church's position in the clearest and, many said, most rigid terms possible. The Cardinal did not believe in "watering down" Church teaching. If a reporter genuinely didn't understand, he would explain things in the simplest possible terms. But when he perceived there was a "hostile agenda" behind the reporter's question, the Cardinal was absolutely uncompromising in his defense of the truth.

That made Father T's Sicilian blood boil. He had no use for the news media's anti-Catholic biases. And he was offended that his archbishop was treated so disrespectfully. "I told the archbishop to retain a PR firm (the one the unions use) to defend the Catholic Church and set the record straight," Father T said frequently. "But he's too kind. He doesn't want to stir things up any more than they already are. That's not the Sicilian way. We fight fire with a blazing inferno, and we know how to handle our enemies in ways they'll never forget!"

"No bishop has ever cared more for his priests and seminarians than the Cardinal did when he was here," Father T always said. "I didn't always agree with him, but he had—and still has—my respect. I always defended him when he was here, and I'll keep on doing it wherever he is!"

"Well, it looks like the Cardinal could use some help

now," Father Mike said. "In spite of the sketchy details, there's no question the Cardinal is in big trouble."

"I'll find out what the heck is going on," Father T said, "if I have to go to Rome myself and turn the Vatican inside out."

"Don't buy your ticket just yet, Sal. Let's both make some phone calls and see if we can find out what the real story is."

"OK, Mike. I'm going to start with my friend Bill Leone. He was my classmate in the seminary, and his first assignment was right here at St. Roch. After many years in parishes, in the school office, in campus ministry and on the staff of our own seminary, he became a very popular spiritual director for the North American College in Rome. Although he's retired now and living with his sister here in the city, he has all kinds of connections in the Vatican. He's bound to know someone who can tell us more."

"Sounds good, Sal. I'll try my friend at the Knights of the Holy Sepulchre's headquarters in Rome. Maybe he can tell us something—or at least point us in the right direction."

"Thanks, Mike. I have to finish the ladies' dinner first, and then meet with the young man who wants to become Catholic, but I'll start making calls as soon as I clean up and go upstairs to my sitting room. Call me if you hear anything more, and I'll do the same."

DAY ONE.
EVENING.

After the ladies had been served and all the cooking utensils in the rectory kitchen had been cleaned and put away (the ladies washed their own dishes and serving bowls in the parish hall's kitchen), Father T met with his would-be Catholic. The young man had completed the reading assignment Father T had given him and had several questions. He was eager to learn more about the teaching and practice of the Church. After about 30 minutes of instruction and discussion, Father T went upstairs to his private sitting room and fireplace for the night. His first call was to his friend Bill.

Msgr. Bill Leone was a man who knew the Vatican from the inside out. Although he was now retired at the age of 82 (two months older than Father T), for many years, he served as a spiritual director for the American seminary in Rome, the North American College (or NAC).

"Have you heard anything about the Cardinal?" Father T asked without engaging in any chitchat.

"Yes, Sal. I just got off the phone with the Vatican's Secretary of State. He says the Holy See's security office picked up two threats against the Cardinal's life from an organization that has its headquarters in Northern Europe but has cells all over the world including here in the United States."

"Northern Europe? What do these folks have against

the Cardinal?" Father T asked.

"Well, from what I understand, they're a group of left-wing terrorists who believe that the Catholic Church is a serious impediment to their progressive, socialist agenda. Outspoken Church leaders like the Cardinal are their sworn enemies. They've vowed to eliminate their opponents one by one as a way of frightening the Church into changing its positions or at least softening its rhetoric."

"That's ridiculous," Father T said. "The Church will never water down its teaching to appease a bunch of socialist bullies. Haven't they ever heard of the martyrs who died for their faith rather than accommodate the demands of godless people—no matter how powerful?"

"I guess not, Sal."

"So what's the Vatican doing about this?"

"The Cardinal is being housed in a private apartment inside the Vatican with 24-hour security. He has everything he needs, but he's not allowed to leave the apartment or talk to anyone except a few of his closest aides. I was told that the Holy Father has spoken to him on the telephone but has not been allowed to visit him personally for security reasons."

"I know that the Cardinal normally walks to work every day (40 minutes each way)," Father T said. "I wonder if he's getting any exercise. I'll bet he's going stir-crazy locked up inside the Vatican. I know I would be."

"You know the Cardinal as well as I do, Sal. He can't be happy about this situation—for lots of reasons. The Vatican is working with the Italian government and Interpol to see if they can find the people responsible for these threats and put a stop to whatever they're planning.

Unfortunately, that could take a very long time."

"This is insanity. We have to do something to help the Cardinal."

"I know how you feel, Sal, but I'm not sure there's anything we can do except pray for his safety."

"I've already entrusted this case to the Sacred Heart—as I always do when I'm faced with tough situations. But I also think we need to do whatever we can to find out who's making these threats and see to it they are stopped once and for all!"

"You know I'll do anything I can to help, Sal. What do you suggest?"

"Let me make some more calls. Then I'll get back to you. One thing I know for sure. I may be 82 years old, but while I have good health and a sound mind, I'm going to use all the gifts God gave me to help my family and friends. The Cardinal was very good to me when he was our archbishop. Now it's payback time. End of story!"

Father T made three more calls that night. The first was to his cousin Msgr. Vincent Cugino, pastor of the Italian parish. The second was to his niece Anna Dominica. Both were horrified to hear about the Cardinal, but both urged Father T not to do anything impulsive.

"Let the authorities handle this, Sal," his cousin said. "There's nothing you can do by yourself."

His niece was even more direct. "Please don't be *un vecchio pazzo* (a crazy old man), Uncle Sal. Don't do anything foolish!"

Father T assured his cousin and his niece that he wouldn't do anything imprudent. Then he called his travel agent, Marisa, and had her book him on the next available flight to Rome.

DAY TWO.
MORNING.

Marisa had been Father T's travel consultant for many years. She knew that he required at least one full day to make all the necessary arrangements—for the care of his elderly and infirm sisters, for covering his Masses and meetings at the parish, and for rescheduling lunch and dinner engagements with friends and community leaders. Marisa also knew she could not book Father T on just any flight to Rome. He had to be comfortable with the route (never through Atlanta!) and with the time allotted for layovers (no running through airports for close connections!). He also insisted on flying business class in spite of the extra expense. "I'm spending my nieces' and nephews' inheritance," he always said. "They can have whatever's left."

Marisa was a real pro with lots of experience and, more importantly, many invaluable connections in the travel industry. She was able to book Father T on a flight that left two days after he called her and that met all his requirements. Per his instructions, the return was "open."

"You're doing what?" Msgr. Cugino said when Father T called him after his morning Mass.

"I'm going to Rome tomorrow."

"I thought you said you wouldn't do anything foolish."

"There's nothing foolish about me going to Rome. After all, I'm a Roman Catholic priest!" Father T said. "As you well know, I've been there 38 times! I certainly know my way around the city."

"Yes, but what are you going to do when you get there?"

"I'm going to find out what's going on with the Cardinal, and I'm going to see if I can help."

Msgr. Cugino was not pleased, but he knew that once Father T made up his mind there was nothing anyone could do about it. "It's a Sicilian thing, I know," he frequently said to his older cousin. "But I'm Sicilian, too," Msgr. Cugino said, "and my advice is: Don't do it."

"Well, please call me every day. And, please don't do or say anything you'll regret. The Cardinal's life is at stake here—and maybe yours, too."

"I'll be careful, Vinnie. I just can't stand by and see the Cardinal suffer this way. It's not right!"

Later that morning, Father T visited the nursing home where his sister Jenny lived. He told her he would be away for a while but, of course, he didn't say why. While he was there, he reminded the nuns who took care of Jenny that while he was away, his niece Anna was empowered to make any necessary decisions.

After he said goodbye to Jenny, Father T stopped at the nearby parish of St. Mary Magdalen to visit his good friend Msgr. John Dutzow. The monsignor had recently retired from his administrative work at the chancery, and he was enjoying his newfound freedom as a full-time pastor.

"I loved my work with youth ministers, coaches and referees," he said. "But I hated the diocesan bureaucracy. I wouldn't go back to that for love or money. Like most pastors, all I want now is to be left alone!"

Father T was pleased to see his friend and former associate so relaxed. The last year of his work at the chancery had been an extremely tense and unhappy time for Msgr. Dutzow. "He should have quit that job two years earlier," Father T said. "But he's too stubborn. He committed to a term of office, and he insisted on fulfilling his commitment no matter what. That's the way priests in our generation were trained. You do what you're asked to do whether you like it or not."

Msgr. John greeted his friend with a smile. "I have coffee and fresh homemade pastry in the kitchen—courtesy of one of my favorite parishioners. Mary is 90 years old, but she still lives alone and does her own cooking and housework. She also walks to Mass every morning—rain or shine. Once a week she brings me some bakery."

Normally the two priests would engage in light conversation—bantering the way priests do when they're comfortable with each other. But this morning Father T had serious news to tell his friend.

Msgr. Dutzow felt very close to the Cardinal, and the news about his "house arrest" at the Vatican because of ominous death threats was very troubling to the monsignor.

"I just can't believe it," Msgr. Dutzow said. "I knew that the Cardinal had enemies, but I can't believe anyone would want to hurt him. He's such a gentle and gracious man."

"The radical left makes no allowances for personalities," Father T said. "With them it's all ideology all the time. You're either with them or they're against you!"

"I know, but still ... I just can't believe it."

"I'm leaving for Rome tomorrow," Father T said. "I'm going to make sure the authorities there are doing everything possible to track these terrorists down and prevent them from doing any harm to the Cardinal or anyone else."

"Gosh, Sal, I wish I could go with you, but right now I have no one to cover for me here at the parish. Since they took my priest in residence away, I've had a very difficult time finding anyone to say Mass for me on the weekends. When I'm away during the week, instead of daily Mass, one of our permanent deacons leads a prayer service and distributes communion. I had to plan months ahead to get a retired priest to say the weekend Masses for me when I lead that pilgrimage next spring."

"I understand, John. I wouldn't ask you to leave your parish right now. I'm fortunate I still have a priest in residence—and a secretary, principal and maintenance man who are fully capable of running the parish while I'm away. Of course, I take my cell phone with me and call home every day."

"I still can't believe this is happening to the Cardinal. When you see him, please let him know he is in my prayers."

"I will, John. And I'll call you from Rome and let you know how it's going."

Father T's next stop was a lunch meeting at the Osteria. He had an appointment with a young priest who a year earlier was falsely accused of sexual misconduct. Father T knew the young man who made the accusation, and he was able to get him to sign an affidavit completely exonerating the young priest. A year later, the priest was having other difficulties, and he was once again reaching out to Father T, who was old enough to be his great uncle, for help.

"Good afternoon, Monsignor. It's a pleasure to see you again. Thank you for agreeing to meet with me."

"As I told you the last time, Father, we're here to help each other. Let's order lunch first. We can talk afterward."

The staff at the Osteria knew exactly what Father T wanted. An Arnold Palmer (half iced tea and half lemonade) and a mixed green salad with house dressing and a full basket of bread sticks (the kind with sesame seeds). The young priest remembered how much he enjoyed the sole ferri the last time he was with Father T, so he ordered it with a glass of white wine.

During the meal, Father T was interrupted several times by former parishioners from the Italian neighborhood.

"When are you coming back to St. Ambrose?" they all asked. "We miss you."

His standard reply was, "I'm there several times a week for funerals and other parish functions, and of course I always come for the *Tavola di San Giuseppe* (St. Joseph's Table, an annual parish festival celebrating the Feast of St. Joseph)."

"We'll see you then, Father. God bless you!"

Finally, the restaurant emptied out, and Father T was left alone with his young guest. "How can I help you, Father?"

"I think I'm having a crisis of faith, Father. I'm no longer sure what I believe. I go through the motions saying my daily prayers, celebrating Mass and doing my work at the parish, but the special feeling I used to have just isn't there anymore. I asked my pastor if I could make a 30-day retreat with the Jesuits to see if I could rekindle my dwindling sense of spirituality, but he says he can't afford to be without me for that long. You know that with 4,000 families we're the largest parish in the archdiocese."

"Your pastor's right, Father, and not just for practical reasons. You're a diocesan priest, not a Jesuit, and while we all need to get away periodically, we have to find our spirituality within the active ministry we've been called to as diocesan priests. Believe me, I know it's not easy. All of us go through rough patches. I was ordained in 1956, and there are still days when I wonder if it was all worth it. Don't get me wrong, I wouldn't trade my years as a priest for anything, and I truly believe that my faith has grown and deepened over the years. But that doesn't mean I'm free from doubts or temptations. Satan tempts old men very differently than he does you who are young, but his influence is no less powerful. We learn to resist temptation and place our trust in God on a daily basis. Sometimes it works amazingly well, but some days it's really tough."

"Do you ever feel like you're just going through the motions, Monsignor? That you're saying the prayers, or celebrating the sacraments, without really paying attention? It seems sacrilegious to do holy things in a haphazard or half-hearted way."

"Of course, Father. Every priest struggles with this problem. We're sinful human beings, not saints. And the more we understand the beauty and dignity of Christ's gifts, the more we're tempted to despair of our ever being worthy. But remember, Christ knew us before he called us. Just like the apostles who were ordinary men like us with lots of human weaknesses, he knew that we would not be perfect. That's why he gives us his grace—to make up for whatever we lack. We have to trust him—and stay close to him—to do the best we can possibly do as priests who are as human and sinful as the people we serve."

"I understand what you're saying, Monsignor, and I believe you're right, but some days I just can't feel it."

"Feelings are overrated, and very unreliable, young man. You can't feel your way into doing what's right. You just have to do it and then pray that God will give you the grace to understand and accept what's happening inside you."

"Thank you, Monsignor. I really appreciate your taking the time to talk with me this afternoon."

"I'll say it again. We're here to help each other. Please don't be a stranger, Father. You're a good man, and you're working with an outstanding pastor. Watch him closely and imitate him (not in a phony way). He'll show you by his example how to find peace in the work God has given you to do in his name."

"God bless you, Monsignor Turiddu,"

DAY TWO.
AFTERNOON.

Father T spent most of the afternoon packing for his trip to Rome. Ordinarily when he went to Italy he would pack an extra suitcase filled with gifts and clothes to give to his relatives in Sicily. "People give me all these gifts for Christmas, and I can't possible use them all. (How many sweaters can one man wear?) So I save them and bring them with me to Sicily to give to my cousins there. They need them a lot more than I do." This trip he only packed one suitcase, and he limited himself to essentials.

Often when he visited Rome, Father T would stay with his cousins who lived just outside the city. This time he wanted to be close to the Vatican. He had a standing invitation to stay at the Cardinal's residence. The Sisters who served as the Cardinal's housekeepers were thrilled when they learned he was coming. They were keenly aware of Father T's reputation as a problem solver.

"Father, we're so worried," the Sister who was the Cardinal's secretary said to Father T when he called to let her know that he would arrive the next day. "Thank you for coming all this way to help us."

"I'm not sure what I can do, but I'm determined to make sure he's OK. No terrorist group will harm our Cardinal if I have anything to say about it."

Father T interrupted his packing several times to make calls on his cell phone. He kept his voicemail messages brief and to the point. He had other things on mind besides chitchatting.

"Hello, Anna. Did you get my message? I'm going to Rome tomorrow. Please look out for your Aunt Anne and Aunt Jenny. Vince thinks I'm being foolish, but I won't change my mind. The Cardinal needs me, so I'm going. End of story!"

"Vince, can you take me to the airport? My flight leaves at noon, and I'd like to be there 2 hours early. I think you said you have the eight o'clock Mass tomorrow. Please pick me up at 9:30."

"Mike, what have you found out about the Cardinal? I'd like to be as up to date as possible before I take off tomorrow. Call me, please!"

Father Mike was on the other line when his friend and former pastor called, but he returned Father T's call promptly. He didn't have much new information, but he was able to report the name of the terrorist group who had threatened the Cardinal. They called themselves The Sword of Justice, and they did, in fact, have cells in the major cities of Europe, Latin America and the U.S.

"Is there a cell here in our city?" Father T asked.

"I don't think so. I believe the closest one is Chicago."

"See if you can find out what part of the city they're in, Mike. I have friends in Chicago and maybe they can help us out."

"OK, Sal. Please be careful when you're in Rome and don't forget to call me."

"I'll call you every day, Mike. Vince and Anna, too. Don't worry about me. I'll be fine."

When he finished packing, Father T sat down in his

sitting room and turned on his satellite TV's Italian channel. The program was some kind of soap opera that he had
no interest in at all, but he watched it anyway because it
helped him keep his Italian up to date. "My mother never
did learn English, so we always spoke Italian at home," he
often said. "But ours was a Sicilian dialect that my parents
brought with them from Sicily more than 100 years ago.
It's important for me to stay current with the language as
it's spoken throughout Italy today."

After he had had as much of the Italian soap opera
as he could stand, Father T said his prayers. His formal
breviary prayers came first, followed by a scripture reading
and *lectio divina* (mediation on a word or phrase from
the reading). Then he spoke directly to the Sacred Heart
of Jesus.

"Anna thinks I'm crazy, Lord. What do you think? Am
I acting foolishly going to Rome to help the Cardinal?
I know most men my age wouldn't do this—or couldn't
do it—but dammit I have to use the good health you've
given me to help the Cardinal. Is that so wrong? Tell me if
you want me to stay home, but do it quickly! I'm already
packed (as you know) and all the arrangements are made.
Unless you give me a sign and tell me otherwise, I'm
getting on that plane tomorrow."

From long experience, Father T knew that when he
prayed to the Sacred Heart he needed to say what he
meant as bluntly as possible. But he also knew it was
important to listen. So he sat quietly in his chair and, as
best he could, he opened his mind and heart to the Lord.

"Praying is 90 percent listening," he always said. "I'm a
much better talker than listener, but if I'm going to hear

what the Sacred Heart has to tell me, I have to shut up after I've had my say and pay attention."

During his quiet moments after speaking his mind to the Sacred Heart, Father T felt the presence of the Lord. He remembered his lunchtime conversation with the young priest, and he asked the Sacred Heart to reveal himself to that young man and let him experience the consolation of his presence. He also formed a clear image in his mind of the Cardinal who had been so good to him and of the loneliness and fear he must be feeling as a virtual prisoner in the Vatican.

"Time's up, Lord," he said abruptly. "In the absence of any contrary indication from you, I'm going to Rome tomorrow. Stay with me, Lord, and with the Cardinal. We both need your help—now more than ever!"

DAY TWO.
EVENING.

Msgr. Vincent Cugino had been pastor of the Italian parish for nearly 15 years. He was an award-winning preacher and a pastor who looked for ways to engage his parishioners in the life of their parish. Father T complained that his younger cousin attended too many meetings, especially during the evening, but Msgr. Cugino insisted that he enjoyed the interaction with his people. Of course, when combined with all the weddings and funerals that he celebrated—almost daily—there was no question that Msgr. Cugino was one of the busiest pastors in the archdiocese.

Father T worried about his cousin's health. Msgr. Cugino had high blood pressure and other stress-related issues, and he very rarely took any time off. Father T himself kept a more active schedule than many priests half his age, but at least he knew how to pace himself, and he rarely did anything that he didn't want to do.

"I'm 82 years old," he reminded his cousin and his friends—most of whom were 15–20 years younger. "I do things my way or not at all!"

Msgr. Cugino and Msgr. Dutzow both canceled their plans for the evening so they could join Father T for dinner at the Osteria. Father Mike joined them, but he said he was on a strict diet and wouldn't be eating. Father T's classmate Msgr. Bill Leone and two laymen who were good friends of Father T also joined the group. They all wanted to express their concern for the Cardinal—and their hopes for Father T's safe return from his unexpected trip to Rome.

The Osteria was one of three restaurants operated by the Norcini family in the city's south end. The house risotto and sole ferri—to name just two of the superb dishes on the Osteria menu—were unparalleled anywhere in the world. Father Mike's strict diet required extraordinary will power given all the seductive temptations presented to him by the Osteria.

"I have news," Father Mike said. "This afternoon I spoke with my friend at the Knights of the Holy Sepulchre in Rome. He says that Interpol has some new intel on three members of The Sword of Justice who've been living in Rome for the past 6 months. They're not Italians; they're Scandinavians, and they're said to be virulent in their hatred for the Catholic Church."

"I don't get it," Msgr. Dutzow said. "So they hate the Church. Fine. But why threaten the Cardinal? What does that accomplish?"

"Well, according to my friend," Father Mike said, "before he received these death threats, the Cardinal was scheduled to represent the Holy See at a meeting of the top leaders of the European Union in Brussels. His topic was to be: *Christianity: Europe's Hope for the Future.* As long as he's locked away at the Vatican, that talk will never happen."

Msgr. Dutzow wasn't buying it. "That makes no sense," he said. "There's nothing to stop the Vatican from pub-lishing the Cardinal's prepared remarks, and the fact that his life is being threatened by terrorists will generate much more media attention than a talk to the European Union would ordinarily."

"With all due respect, Monsignor, that's where you're wrong." It was Father T's friend Msgr. Leone speaking out for the first time. "The Vatican doesn't want any publicity right now—especially in the wake of the sex abuse scandals that have recently shaken so many European countries. The terrorists have the Church between a rock and a hard place. Either the Vatican keeps everything quiet and misses an important opportunity to evangelize the EU leaders. Or they tell the world that one of their most outspoken cardinals is hiding in the Vatican because of a left-wing terrorist threat."

"This is insanity," Father T said with more than a little disgust. "We don't give in to terrorists. Period. How can we effectively proclaim the New Evangelization if we're afraid to speak the truth? The Vatican knows this. There must be more going on here than meets the eye. When I get over there, I'm going to get to the bottom of this."

"What's your plan, Sal?" Msgr. Leone asked. "And what can we do to help?"

"My plan is to dig around the Vatican and see what I can learn 'off the record.' Then I'm going to find a way to see the Cardinal and find out how he's doing. I also want to discover what he knows about The Sword of Justice. Once I have a clearer picture of what's actually going on there, I'm going to see what I can do to stop the terrorists and let the Cardinal go home to his residence on the Via Conciliazione!"

Msgr. Cugino was visibly disturbed. "Don't get ahead

of yourself, Sal. You're not Vatican security or Interpol. If you interfere in the wrong places at the wrong time, you could end up making things worse for the Cardinal—and for yourself."

"I know, Vinnie. And I appreciate the concern that all of you are showing for my welfare and for the Cardinal. The Sacred Heart is my constant companion. He will keep me out of harm's way."

"Good night, Sal," Msgr. Leone said, "and have a safe trip. Let's all plan to get together here when you return. We'll laugh and raise a toast to our friend the Cardinal."

" Goodbye, Father!" said the two laymen.

"Italians don't say goodbye," Father T replied. We say, "*Arrivederci!* Until we meet again!"

DAY THREE.
MORNING.

Father T always said the 7:15 a.m. weekday Mass in the chapel on the second floor of the school building. It saved on heating and air conditioning costs in the church. A half dozen parishioners—most of them regulars—joined him. During the brief homily, Father T mentioned that he was leaving for Rome "on Church business" and that he hoped to be back in a week or two.

After Mass, two of his good friends and faithful parishioners, Joe and Rosemary Lindell, asked if there was anything wrong. They knew it was very unusual for Father T to leave the parish so abruptly—especially to return to Italy. Ordinarily his visits to Sicily and Rome were planned months in advance. At first they wondered if one of his relatives was ill or in trouble, but when he said he was going on "Church business," they were understandably confused. What kind of Church business would take an ordinary American pastor (even one with Father T's reputation) to Rome so unexpectedly?

Father T apologized for appearing secretive, but he assured his friends that his mission was an important one and that he hoped to complete it successfully and return as soon as possible. Rosemary and Joe had been Father T's parishioners for many years. He had baptized their children and grandchildren. They knew him well enough not to press him. He requested their prayers, and they promised they would pray for him at Mass every day while he was away.

"Would you like a ride to the airport, Father?" Joe asked.

"Thank you, Joe, but Msgr. Cugino is picking me up at 9:30."

"God bless you, Father," Rosemary said. "Please return to us safely."

Father T's usual breakfast was coffee, cereal and one slice of toasted Italian bread with sesame seeds. With breakfast, he always read the newspaper (which he derided as "that rag") beginning with the obituaries. He was relieved to see that the only deaths he recognized that morning were two parishioners from the Italian parish whose families were relatively new to the city and who, therefore, would not expect him to join their pastor for the funeral Mass. (Father T refused to be the principal celebrant or give the homily during funerals of his former parishioners at the Italian parish. "That's the pastor's role," he insisted. "I'll say the final prayers over the body and give the final blessing.")

Father T was especially pleased to see that in this edition of the newspaper there was no mention of the Cardinal or anything related to the Vatican or the archdiocese. He remembered the vicious stories and scathing editorials that were a regular occurrence when the Cardinal was the archbishop. The local news media had been rigidly intolerant of the Cardinal's position on denying Holy Communion to government officials or other high-profile persons who failed to uphold, or who publicly opposed, moral issues that the Cardinal argued are not peculiar to Catholic teaching but are "written on every human heart." The media tried to cast the Cardinal's position as imposing Catholic morality on the general population, but he stead-fastly refused to accept that narrow characterization of his stand on these important moral issues. Father T probably wouldn't have taken such a strong stand personally, but he supported his archbishop absolutely, and he resented the news media's arrogant and sanctimonious pronounce-ments on issues they couldn't possibly understand.

After breakfast, Father T had brief meetings with his secretary, his principal and his maintenance man. By the time his cousin arrived—exactly at 9:30—Monsignor Salvatore E. Turiddu was all packed and ready to return to his beloved Italy—this time on serious Church business.

As the plane took off, it ascended slowly over the city that Father T loved. The day was clear and sunny, so he was able to see many of the neighborhoods that were familiar to him after 57 years of active parish ministry. A lot had changed in the city—and in the Church—during those nearly six decades. A massive exodus from the city to the suburbs driven by "white flight" had completely changed the city's demographics. The Church followed its people—building new parishes and schools in the county and beyond, while leaving magnificent old churches and schools to face declining populations and severe financial shortages.

Father T's response was to earn a master's degree in urban planning and organize his people—families who lived in the Italian neighborhood—to resist the insanity of wholesale out-migration and the senseless abandonment of their homes and neighborhoods. "If you don't panic, and if you refuse to sell your homes, no one can take them from you," was Father T's consistent refrain from the pulpit and at community meetings. "Let's stick together to keep our neighborhood strong!"

The strategy worked. Now, nearly 50 years later, the Italian neighborhood was thriving—a great place to live and raise children and a tourist attraction known for its wonderful shops and restaurants. The Italian parish, now led by Father T's cousin, was one of the strongest churches in the city with a vibrant parish community, an excellent school and money in the bank!

As a result of his efforts on behalf of the Italian neighborhood and his beloved city, Father T earned the title "*il salvatore della città*, (the savior of the city)." As recently as a year earlier, when the then 81-year-old priest helped solve a mystery that prevented a domestic terrorist threat that would have cost hundreds of lives and embarrassed law enforcement at local, state and national levels, the mayor had once again publicly thanked Father T for saving the city from disaster.

What hadn't changed over the years was Father T's passion for the people he served or his commitment to the city that was the only home he had ever known. He always said he was "a city pastor." When he was forced to leave the city limits to attend archdiocesan meetings or to preside at weddings or funerals in the suburbs, he felt totally out of his element.

A previous archbishop once offered to appoint Father T pastor of a wealthy suburban parish, but he respectfully declined. "I wouldn't feel comfortable there," he said. When asked why not, Father T's response was simple: "No alleys."

Gazing out the window, Father T recalled all the planning meetings he conducted over the years with his two colleagues—now deceased—in the archdiocese's Office of Urban Planning. Dr. George Durban was a demographer whose knowledge of statistics and complex data was extraordinary. In the days before ready access to personal computers or mobile devices, George did mapping and analysis in his head. And his predictions were always accurate.

Lou Lombardy, on the other hand, was a political strategist. He never ran for public office but, instead, was content to work behind the scenes. He knew every major player in the city, and he identified every political and economic movement before it happened.

When Father T, George and Lou met with a city pastor to give him advice about his parish or neighborhood, you could be sure that the information was accurate and the advice was sound. Unfortunately, officials at the chancery didn't always consult the Office of Urban Planning before making decisions. As a result, parishes and schools were closed in areas of the city that needed them badly, and properties were sold for far less than their value. That made Father T's Sicilian blood boil. He could never understand why his brother priests, and their bishops, failed to heed the advice of laymen like Lou Lombardy and Dr. George Durban who were wholly dedicated to the Church and who knew their business better than any clergyman could.

Now George and Lou were both gone. Pastors still called Father T for advice on planning matters, and the current archbishop made a point of consulting him on a wide range of issues, but the glory days of urban planning were long past.

An announcement by the pilot that the plane had reached its cruising altitude—allowing him to turn off the "fasten seat belts" sign—interrupted Father T's reflections. He stood up and removed his suit coat and Roman collar. His practice was always to wear his collar while boarding the airplane so that the flight attendants and passengers knew he was a priest. Once he had established that fact, he allowed himself to travel more comfortably. This was a short flight to Chicago where he would connect to an Alitalia flight nonstop to Rome. During his layover, he planned to make some phone calls to friends and family in the Chicago area—especially to inquire about this strange outfit known as The Sword of Justice.

Marisa had made sure that Father T had plenty of time between flights. He walked down the long concourse carrying his overnight bag. Once he arrived at the departure gate, he found a seat and began making phone calls. None of his Chicago family members or friends had ever heard of The Sword of Justice, but John Vitale, a retired policeman who had served with Father T on the Italian-American Council, which met in Chicago for two days every summer, offered to call a friend at Homeland Security who might have more current information about terrorists groups.

"My cell phone works in Italy, Giovanni," Father T said. "I went into the AT&T store in my neighborhood and had them activate international calling." I'll be unreachable for 9 or 10 hours during the flight, but you can call me any time after that." His friend assured him he would call as soon as he had any information to share.

About five minutes before boarding for business class was set to begin, Father T's cell phone vibrated in his shirt pocket. As he looked at the caller ID, he was surprised to see that it was his archbishop. Father T had called the archbishop as Msgr. Cugino was driving him to the airport. The message he left on the boss's voicemail was not very detailed.

"I'm going to Italy for a week or two, Archbishop," his message said. "I'll call you when I return."

Father T had been happy that the archbishop didn't answer his phone. He really didn't want to have to explain what his plans were—fearing that the archbishop might not approve.

"I got your message, Monsignor," the archbishop said. "Where are you now?"

"I'm at O'Hare airport just about to board my flight to Rome."

"I'm glad I caught you. I want to wish you a safe flight, but I also want to urge you to be prudent in your dealings with the Vatican and Interpol. We don't need an international incident, and we especially don't want anything to happen to you or to the Cardinal."

"I've got the Sacred Heart on my side, Archbishop. He has always taken care of me."

"I know that, Monsignor, but I also know that our Lord also expects us to take good care of ourselves. Don't forget what you always say to people who seek your advice: *You have to know the territory!* When you get to Rome, in spite of your many trips to Italy and your friends and family there, you will be in unfamiliar territory. Don't make the mistake of thinking you're on solid ground."

"I know, Archbishop. That's good advice. I promise to be careful—and I'll keep you informed of my activities."

"Call me anytime, Monsignor, and give my best to the Cardinal. Assure him that he is in our prayers."

"I will, Archbishop. Thank you for calling."

"*Buon viaggio*, Monsignor Turiddu. God be with you."

Once he boarded the plane, and was settled into a seat in business class with plenty of legroom, Father T closed his eyes. By the time he opened them again, he would be halfway across the Atlantic Ocean on his way to the Eternal City.

DAY THREE.
EVENING.

While Father T slept, (it was only 5 p.m. in Chicago, but midnight in Rome) his friend the Cardinal was engaged in a very unpleasant conversation with a representative of the Vatican's security service and an agent from Interpol's office in Rome. The subject was a new death threat that contained information about the Cardinal's specific location in the Apostolic Palace. The only way the terrorists could have known where the Cardinal was being housed was if someone inside the Vatican leaked that information.

"*Eminenza,*" the Interpol agent said, "ordinarily Interpol does not get involved in religious matters, but because we believe that a terrorist organization is responsible for these threats against an official of the Vatican City State, we have decided to assist the Vatican's security service in protecting you and the Holy See from this terrorist group. Unfortunately, we cannot guarantee your safety here in the Vatican. The terrorists have an inside connection, and until we find out who is giving them information, it's too dangerous for you to stay here."

"Where do you propose that I go?" the Cardinal asked.

"There is a Benedictine monastery in Umbria—the *Monastero di San Benedetto* in Norcia, the birthplace of St. Benedict. It is so remote that no one would think to look for you there," the Vatican official said. "We think it is a much safer place for you to be."

"Safer than the Vatican? That's hard to believe. I don't know what information has been leaked to the terrorists, but surely you can find a way to protect me here."

"No, your Eminence. We cannot," said the Interpol agent. "It's too much of a risk for you. And, of course, we must also think about the Holy Father's safety. A terrorist attack inside the walls of the Vatican would be devastating for the Holy See—especially if the pope were harmed in any way."

"I certainly don't want any harm to come to His Holiness," the Cardinal said. "And I don't want to be the proximate cause for a terrorist attack here in the Vatican. But are you sure Norcia is the best place for me? I know the prior of the monastery there. He is a good and holy man, but I doubt that he or his monks are prepared to deal with this kind of situation. They are simple men who celebrate Mass in the Extraordinary Form and pray the Divine Office in Latin in strict observance of the Holy Rule. They will not appreciate the kind of distractions my presence will inevitably bring to their ordered way of life. Besides, I've visited there, and I know the monastery buildings are very crowded. I doubt they will have room for me."

"We have spoken with the prior, *Eminenza*," the Vatican official said. "He reminded us that St. Benedict counseled his monks to receive guests as they would Christ himself. He said the monks would be honored to have you stay with them for as long as you wish and that they will make room for you in spite of their crowded conditions. We assured him that your stay will be no longer than absolutely necessary."

"When do you want me to leave?" the Cardinal asked.

"Tomorrow morning," said the Interpol agent. "We're

making the necessary arrangements to transport you. No one inside the Vatican will know where we are taking you, and the route will be kept secret from everyone but ourselves."

"I'm truly sorry to cause so much trouble for everyone—especially the Holy Father and members of his household. My grateful prayers are with you, gentlemen. *Mille grazie.*"

IL QUARTO GIORNO

IL QUARTO GIORNO.
MATTINATA.
(Day Four. Morning)

The Alitalia flight from Chicago arrived in Rome on time, and the weary passengers disembarked and then lined-up to go through Italian passport control. The lines for citizens of European Union countries moved quickly. Lines for all others took more time, but Father T considered himself lucky to be able to get to baggage claim and retrieve his luggage in less than 20 minutes. He was pleased to see that bags from the Chicago flight were already on the conveyor belt, and he quickly spotted his well-worn suitcase making its way around the belt.

Father T grabbed his suitcase and started for the signs marked *Uscita* (exit) and *Dogana* (customs) when he realized that the handle on his suitcase was broken. Since he couldn't pull out the handle, he would have to carry the suitcase rather than wheel it. Fortunately, he was in good health and had packed lighter than usual.

Since he had nothing to declare to customs, he walked quickly through the exit doors to the main concourse of the international terminal where hundreds of people were waiting to greet family members and friends returning to Rome. Limo drivers held signs with the names of passengers who had reserved cars to take them to local destinations.

When he was younger, Father T used to bypass this crowd and head straight to the escalators that took passengers up to railway station. Trains to Rome's *Stazione Termini* were inexpensive and left Da Vinci Airport frequently for the 30-minute trip to the city's main terminal near the church of *Santa Maria Maggiore* and the baths of the Emperor Diocletian. The taxi ride from the train station to the Vatican was a short distance, but during rush hours it could take a very long time and become quite expensive. The number 64 bus from the train station to St. Peter's Square was always an option, but it was very crowded. (Years earlier, Father T's cousins had shown him how to safely take the bus—by leaving his fancy briefcase at home and packing his guidebook and other papers in a plastic grocery bag that no one would suspect contained anything of value!)

Fortunately, Father T's friend Msgr. Leone had arranged for a Vatican driver to meet him and take him to the Cardinal's residence. "The driver will assume you are a bishop," his friend told him. "Don't correct him. And don't try to tip him. He's a professional driver not a cabbie. He'll be offended if you try to give him money."

The driver was there waiting for him with a sign that simply said "Turiddu," but as Msgr. Leone had warned him, the driver clearly thought he was a bishop and insisted on calling him *Eccellenza* (Your Excellency). Father T nodded and smiled—as though he didn't understand Italian—and rode comfortably to the Vatican in a black Mercedes Benz sedan.

It was a cool October morning, but the sun was shining, and it promised to be a beautiful day in the Eternal City.

Father T couldn't help thinking about his first trip to Rome more than 57 years earlier during the summer following his ordination to the diaconate. He and a friend, a fellow deacon also in his final year before ordination to the priesthood, had traveled to Europe by steamship. All their travel arrangements had been made by their pastor at the time (affectionately called "the boss"). The boss had spent many years in Rome studying, and then teaching canon law before coming home and being appointed pastor of the Italian parish. He mapped out for them all the sights they should see during their first trip to Rome. He also used his contacts at the Vatican to arrange an audience with Pope Pius XII and give them access to places in the Apostolic Palace and Vatican Gardens that most people didn't even know existed.

Rome was a very different place back then. The city was still recovering from the Second World War, and there was wide-scale poverty and unemployment. Political unrest was a way of life then, and the government of Italy seemed to change every six months, causing chaos and constant anxiety for Father T's relatives in Sicily and Rome. And yet, in some ways things were calmer in those days than today. Father T recalled driving a rental car across the *Piazza San Pietro* right up to the steps of St. Peter's Basilica. That could never happen now. Especially since the attempted assassination of Pope John Paul II in 1981, no unauthorized vehicles were allowed in the square or anywhere near the basilica. Today, Swiss Guards tightly controlled access to the Vatican offices. Security cameras were everywhere, and they were carefully monitored by specially trained members of the Vatican's security team.

Traffic was moderate on the *Autostrada* and the Via Aurelia, and they made good time coming into the city. Things changed once they approached the Vatican. October is always crowded with pilgrims, and the fact that seven new saints were about to be canonized added to the numbers of international visitors to the Holy See. The World Synod of Bishops taking place that month called for heightened security because of the unusually large number of cardinals and bishops from all over the world who were attending this historic gathering. Their topic was the "New Evangelization"—spreading the Gospel of Jesus Christ to those who have never known him but also to those nominal Christians who have been so influenced by modern secularism that they need to experience his saving power once again with a new freshness and immediacy! Shortly before he left home, Father T had approved a letter to all his parishioners outlining the parish's activities for the Year of Faith and urging them to accept the Holy Father's call to be evangelizers in their families and neighborhoods.

The driver arrived at the Cardinal's residence on the Via Conciliazione just as two large tour buses were letting out their passengers. It was impossible to turn into the alley where the entrance was located, so the driver stopped behind the buses (adding to the congestion) and motioned to Father T to get out. The driver removed "the bishop's" overnight bag and damaged suitcase from the trunk of the black Mercedes and escorted his passenger through the crowd of pilgrims to the apartment building's side entrance. He pressed the buzzer and announced to security guard that the Cardinal's guest had arrived. The door was opened immediately and the guard welcomed Father T, warmly taking his luggage and showing him to the small elevator that would take him to the Cardinal's 5th floor apartment.

Once he got off the elevator on the 5th floor, Father T was greeted by two nuns wearing the distinctive habit of their Order. One was the Cardinal's secretary; the other was his housekeeper.

"Oh, Father, we're so happy you're here!" the Cardinal's secretary exclaimed. "We think they've removed His Eminence from the Vatican and taken him someplace. No one will tell us where he is or how long he'll be away."

"When did this happen?" Father T asked, "and how did you find out about it?"

"A man from the Vatican's security team came here early this morning—before our 7 a.m. Mass—and handed us a note from the Cardinal. It included a list of books and clothing items that His Eminence asked we give to the note's bearer. We were told not to ask questions but to simply "pray for me" and for "a speedy resolution of this unfortunate situation." In conclusion, the Cardinal's note said that he would be away "for an indeterminate period of time but would return as soon as it was safe to do so."

"Of course, we did as His Eminence asked," the Cardinal's secretary said. "We gathered his things and resisted the very strong temptation to ask lots of questions!"

"I'll get to the bottom of this, Sisters," Father T promised. "Please don't worry about the Cardinal. I'm sure he's in good hands."

The housekeeper showed Father T to the guest room of the Cardinal's handsome apartment. She assured him that her staff would provide for all his needs as long as he stayed with them as a guest of the Cardinal. "All we ask is that you let us know when you plan to go out for meals," the housekeeper said. "Otherwise we'll prepare meals for you here." Sister then gave Father T a set of keys—one for the side entrance to the building and one for the apartment—and a sheet of paper that described in detail the *horarium* (daily schedule) of the Cardinal's household including morning prayers, Mass, meal times and evening prayer with Benediction of the Blessed Sacrament. Guests also received instructions for having laundry done by the household staff and for placing special dietary needs for meals. Finally, guests were given the password for the computer in the library and instructions on how to connect to the Internet.

POMERIGGIO.

The Sisters served Father T a hearty meal (*pranzo*) of pasta, veal, vegetables and salad. Then they gave him time to rest (*siesta*). Before he lay down, the priest asked the Cardinal's secretary if she could arrange an appointment with the Prefect of the Papal Household for later that afternoon or evening. He wanted to begin his investigation immediately, and there was no better place to start than by talking to the monsignor who was responsible for day-to-day life in the Vatican.

Father T opened his well-worn breviary and quickly said his prayers. He made a special point of asking the Sacred Heart to guide him as he searched for ways to help his friend the Cardinal. He also remembered his sisters at home and the many family members and friends—living and deceased—who supported him in his priestly ministry. "Lord, you do so many good things with weak and foolish men like me. Help me be of service to you here in Rome. Or, as Vinnie would say, at least keep me from getting in the way and making a bad situation worse!"

It didn't take long for the 82-year-old priest to close his eyes and begin to dream. He found himself in the old neighborhood with his brothers. They were sitting outside at a table in the yard behind the tenement building that was their home. His brothers were arguing playfully about sports and city politics. Father T knew he was dreaming, but he was happy for the chance to be with his older brothers again. All of them were gone now—even Dominic, the oldest, who was 91 when he died suddenly after never being sick a day in his life. Dom always looked out for Father T (and every member of his family). He ran the family's very successful business, and he used the profits wisely to make sure that his parents and siblings were fully provided for. Father T missed him ... .

As he dreamed, Father T heard a gentle tapping that he couldn't identify. He opened his eyes and gradually recognized the sound. Someone was knocking, very softly, on the guest room door.

"Sister, is that you?"

"Yes, Father," the Cardinal's secretary said from behind the guest room door. "I'm very sorry to disturb you, but the Prefect of the Papal Household will see you this afternoon at 4:30. I thought you might need some time to get ready."

Father T looked at his wristwatch—a gift from his brother Dominic—and saw that it was nearly 3:30 p.m. (8:30 a.m. back home). He wanted to be sure he called home to check on his sisters and let everyone know he arrived safely.

"Thank you, Sister. I'm getting up now."

After a quick shower and shave, Father T put on his best cassock with its purple piping and sash. It was something he rarely wore, but "when in Rome ... ." Being dressed properly was important—especially since he had come on very serious Church business. It also ensured that the Swiss Guards would acknowledge his rank as a member of the papal household (a monsignor) and give him access to areas of the Vatican City State that were off limits to most people.

Glancing at his watch again, Father T decided to make a quick call home before taking the short walk from the cardinal's residence through the *Piazza di San Pietro* to the Bronze Door that was the entrance to the Vatican's Apostolic Palace. He dialed the number remembering to use the country code, but all he got was a recording in Italian saying that there was no service. Father T couldn't understand it. He had made a special trip to the AT&T store in his neighborhood to verify that his cell phone's international calling feature was activated. The young man who waited on him assured him that he would have no difficulty making or receiving calls from anywhere in Italy. No such luck. For now, his cell phone was useless, and he didn't have time to worry about it.

As he hurried out the door, Father T made sure he filled his pockets with small coins. He knew from experience that there were beggars on every street corner, and he couldn't bring himself to pass by without tossing something into each beggar's cup. It was a nuisance, but Father T believed that true charity is always uncomfortable. "If it feels good," he used to say, "it's not sacrificial giving."

The prefect's office had faxed a form to the Cardinal's secretary that would allow Father T to pass through the Swiss Guards and Vatican security and be escorted to a small parlor containing priceless artwork. After waiting no more than five minutes, the prefect entered the parlor with a broad smile and a warm greeting for the distinguished American monsignor whom he knew was a very close friend of the cardinal who was now hidden away in an obscure monastery in Umbria.

The prefect's greeting and the two men's initial conversation was in Italian, but they switched to English as soon as they got down to business.

"Monsignor Turiddu, I understand you've come to inquire about your friend the Cardinal. I'm afraid all I can tell you is that His Eminence is in a secure location and is in no immediate danger."

"Thank you, *Eccelenza*. I respect the need to keep the Cardinal's location a secret, but can you at least tell me more about the threats against him? All we've heard is that a terrorist organization, The Sword of Justice, has placed him on their "hit list" and that Vatican security and Interpol are taking this very seriously."

"You're correct, Monsignor. We are not overreacting. This organization's past activities give us grave reasons to be concerned for the Cardinal's safety. That's why we determined that even the Vatican was not a secure enough location. As you know, recent leaks have shown us that we have much work to do to ensure that sensitive information doesn't fall into the wrong hands. This is especially important when human lives are at stake!"

"Can you tell me why these terrorist thugs have chosen the Cardinal as their target? I know he's considered to be an outspoken conservative churchman, but anyone who knows him can see that he is a kind and gentle man who is deeply committed to preaching the Gospel—no matter how unpopular."

"Your friend is an easy target, Monsignor. It's true that there are other members of the College of Cardinals who are equally outspoken, but they have not captured the kind of media attention in America or Europe that your Cardinal has. Not since the Holy Father was prefect of the

Congregation for the Doctrine of the Faith—where he was nicknamed 'God's Rottweiler'—has anyone in the Vatican received this much vicious treatment at the hands of the radical left!"

"It's outrageous!" Father T exclaimed forgetting for the moment where he was. "I think it's time these *idioti*, and the knuckleheads in the media who support them, were exposed for the fools they truly are!"

"I know how you feel, Monsignor, but it's not that easy. The Synod of Bishops, which is going on now, has devoted many hours to discussing how to deal with our contemporary news and entertainment media and its influence on culture. Your Cardinal has been one of the most vocal critics of the modern media, but he and many others have also argued that we can't simply condemn the media (especially the new social media). We have to fight fire with fire, as you Americans say. That's why the pope now has a Twitter account. He is determined to proclaim the Gospel using every instrument of communication available to him!"

"Thank you, *Eccellenza*. I respect the Holy Father's determination to practice the New Evangelization. At our age, the temptation is to leave *strumenti nuovi* to the young, but wise men like His Holiness take advantage of whatever new instruments God gives them. I've already decided that when I return to the United States I'm going to invest in the iPhone 5!"

"How long will you be with us, Monsignor?"

"Until I'm satisfied that I've done everything I can to help the Cardinal."

"Your prayers are invaluable, Monsignor. Leave the rest

to God."

"I understand what you're saying," Father T said. "The Sacred Heart and I talk about the Cardinal's safety constantly. But I wasn't raised to sit back and wait—not as long as there's any chance I can help. I intend to learn a lot more about The Sword of Justice, and while I promise not to get in the way, I'm going to do whatever I can to help His Eminence come home safely. End of story!"

"You're a brave man, Monsignor Turiddu, and the Cardinal is fortunate to have you as his friend. May Almighty God bless you and keep you from harm."

"*Grazie, Eccellenza.* I promise to keep you informed of my activities—as soon as I find out why my cell phone isn't working!"

IL QUARTO GIORNO.
SERA.
(Day Four. Evening)

Father T was frustrated. His cell phone wouldn't work at all. More importantly, his meeting with the Prefect of the Papal Household, while very cordial, had produced no new information. *Niente!* He might as well have stayed home and let Father Mike and his friend Msgr. Leone work their contacts in the Vatican.

He found a cell phone store on the Via Cola Di Rienzo not far from the Vatican. The young woman who waited on him couldn't do anything to help. Father T was now dressed in casual street clothes, so she addressed him as *Signore*. Sensing his frustration, the young clerk called the store's owner to come and assist her.

"*Parlo italiano fluentemente* (I speak fluent Italian)," Father T said as the man approached the counter. He wanted to make sure the proprietor understood that he could speak freely in Italian and not worry about being misunderstood.

"How can we help you, *Signore?*"

"I'm an American priest. Before I left home, I arranged to have international service activated on my cell phone. Obviously something went wrong because it doesn't work at all. I know I can't call out, and I haven't received any incoming calls since I arrived which is very unusual for me."

The proprietor attempted to install a new sim card, but it didn't help.

"I'm not sure what the problem is, *Padre*, but for some reason your phone won't accept the new card. I'd advise you to wait and have it checked out when you return to the United States."

"But what do I do in the meantime? I really can't afford to be completely cut off from my family and friends back home."

"Not a problem, *Padre*. Why don't you buy a disposable cell phone with prepaid minutes? You'll be able to make calls here in Roma and to America very easily."

"How much will it cost me?"

"Probably less than you're paying for international service on your American cell phone." He quoted the price, and Father T immediately accepted. He would get his money back from AT&T when he returned home and be about $50 ahead in the bargain.

Once his new disposable phone was activated, Father T found an outdoor café on the Via Cola Di Rienzo where he ordered an espresso and began making calls home. He spoke to his secretary at the parish and asked her to send an e-mail with his Italian cell phone number to family members and friends. Then he called his niece Anna, Msgr. Leone, Msgr. Cugino, Msgr. Dutzow and Father Mike. No one answered, so he left the same brief voice mail message each time: "It's me. I arrived safely. My cell phone doesn't work here, so I bought a new one just while I'm here in Italy. The number is +39 347 893 0011. Call me."

From where he sat, Father T could see the Piazza del Risorgimento with its many cars, buses and pedestrians. Someone once told him that during World War II, Mussolini (*Il Duce*) was known to address large crowds from one of the balconies overlooking this public square. Or perhaps it was the Piazza Venezia, which was much closer to the national government's headquarters. He couldn't remember. Jet lag was beginning to set in after the long trip from home, and Father T decided to return to the Cardinal's residence and retire early—following what he hoped would be a very light supper prepared for him by the Sisters.

Many pilgrims were in St. Peter's Square that evening in spite of the fact that the basilica was now closed. The shops were crowded and there was very little room in the cafés that lined the Via Conciliazione, the grand boulevard that extended from the Tiber River to St. Peter's Basilica.

Father T walked slowly toward the Cardinal's residence trying as best he could to avoid the busier streets. As he passed through one of the archways in the wall known as the *Passetto* (once a secret passageway that connected the Vatican with a nearby fortress, the *Castel Sant' Angelo*), he nearly collided with a handsome young man wearing a black cassock.

"Excuse me, Father T. I didn't see you," the young man said in English. "Welcome back to Rome. I know you've been here many times."

"Huh? How do you know me?" was the startled priest's reply.

"I'm a seminarian studying here in Rome at the North American College. I helped out at the cathedral parish last summer, and I sometimes did odd jobs at the archbishop's residence. I met you when you came with two of our retired priests to have lunch with the archbishop. I was one of the seminarians who helped serve lunch."

"I'm very sorry I don't remember you, young man. When you get to be my age you'll understand. What's your name and what parish are you from?"

"It's not a problem, Father. My name is Michael O'Keefe. I grew up in St. Margaret of Scotland Parish, and I went to St. Mary's High School and then to the university. I heard you were here in Rome. All the guys are talking about it. They say you're here to help the Cardinal."

"So much for keeping a low profile," Father T said. "I'm very pleased to meet you for the second time, Mr. O'Keefe. Do you have time for an espresso? I'd like to chat with you about the Cardinal and his current difficulties."

"I'd really like to, Father, but I'm on my way to meet one of my professors. He's helping me with Hebrew. I'm pretty good with languages, but the idiosyncrasies of ancient Hebrew are beyond me. I'd be happy to meet you tomorrow. I have a light class schedule on Thursdays."

"Are you free for lunch? Where should we meet?"

"There's a very nice restaurant at the bottom of the Janiculum Hill called *Sor Eva*—along the Tiber. It's an easy walk for me down the hill from the seminary, and it's not far from the Cardinal's residence."

"I know the place. I'll meet you there at 1:30."

"That's perfect, Father T. Thank you. *Buona sera!*"

The Sisters had supper ready for their guest as soon as he arrived. It wasn't quite as light as he would have liked, but it was well-prepared. "My mother would approve," Father T said to himself. "The pasta is perfect, and the red sauce complements it nicely rather than being too thick or heavily seasoned. Fresh-baked bread, a garden salad and some *dolci* (Italian pastries) completed the meal. One glass of red wine was all Father T allowed himself during dinner. He was eager to retire for the evening, and knew he would have no trouble sleeping at the end of this very long day.

The Monks of Norcia extend their hospitality to the Cardinal

IL QUINTO GIORNO

IL QUINTO GIORNO.
PRIMA MATTINATA.
(Day Five. Early Morning)

It was well after midnight and Father T was sleeping soundly in the Cardinal's guest room—enjoying the comfort of soft sheets, warm blankets and fluffy pillows. The Sisters made sure that he had everything he needed, and he was grateful for their hospitality.

The Cardinal himself was not so fortunate. He tossed and turned on a small, hard bed in a tiny monastic cell that had been set aside for his use. The monastery had no guest room because the community had grown so quickly and every available room was needed—either as a bedroom or for storage space. So, the Cardinal was given the use of a monk's cell located near the monastic library. (The library had been blessed by Cardinal Joseph Ratzinger the year before he was elected pope and took the name Benedict XVI. The pope was a personal benefactor of the community—sending them books from his own collection to add to the monastery library.) Unlike most monks' cells, which had bare floors and no amenities of any kind, the Cardinal's room did have a rug on the floor, an easy chair and a desk and chair for writing—all borrowed from the owners of several hotels and restaurants in the city of Norcia who were among the monks' most generous benefactors.

The monk who gave up his monastic cell for the Cardinal's use was the community's brewmaster—trained by Carthusian monks in Belgium who have been brewing beer for centuries. He placed a simple mattress on the floor of the brewery (originally the monastery's garage) and slept soundly until the bells tolled for Matins at 3:45 a.m.

The Cardinal had no complaints about the way the monks received him. In fact, they extended to him every possible courtesy, going out of their way to ensure his comfort (and his safety). But the Cardinal was not at home in this small, crowded place, which could also be very noisy when there were celebrations in the Piazza di San Benedetto right below the monks' windows, and he prayed for the grace to accept his current situation, with all its minor inconveniences, with the same equanimity that our Lord displayed when he told a would-be disciple "Foxes have dens and birds of the sky have nests, but the Son of Man has nowhere to rest his head" (Mt 8:20).

The monks were very pleased to have the Cardinal as their guest—even under these very difficult circumstances. They considered him a patron because of his strong support for their efforts to revive the monastic tradition begun here in the birthplace of St. Benedict more than 1,000 years ago. (The monastery that was originally founded in the 10th century was forced to close in 1810 because of laws imposed on the monks by the Napoleonic Code. The new community, which was led by a group of Americans, was founded in Rome in 1998 and charged with the responsibility of moving to Norcia to care for the Basilica of San Benedetto—built over the birthplace of St. Benedict and St. Scholastica—and to minister to the many pilgrims who visit there each year.)

For his part, the Cardinal approved of their faithful witness to the strict observance of Benedictine life, and he was pleased to celebrate Mass with them in the Extraordinary Form and to join them for at least some of their hours of prayer. The Cardinal also enjoyed the monks' simple meals accompanied by *Birra Nursia*, the local beer brewed by the monks in their former garage and sold throughout Italy.

It was about 3:30 a.m. when the Cardinal's fitful sleep was abruptly interrupted. Two men wearing ski masks and holding assault rifles nudged him roughly. As he opened his eyes, one of them quickly covered his mouth with a gloved hand to prevent him from speaking.

"Don't make a sound or many people will die," one of the men whispered in thickly accented English. "Get dressed. Quickly!"

"Where are you taking me?" the Cardinal asked.

"We told you not to speak," the gunman answered. "They'll be plenty of time to talk later. Right now we prefer to depart without having to kill anyone."

As he dressed, putting on the plain black suit he wore on the trip from the Vatican to the monastery, the Cardinal wondered about the two Interpol agents who were assigned to guard him and were supposed to be taking turns keeping vigil outside his bedroom door. He hoped that his abductors' desire not to kill anyone applied to them as well!

The two gunmen led the Cardinal through the dark corridor of the monastery to the nearest door marked Uscita. A black SUV was waiting in an alley just outside the monastery's small courtyard with a third masked man in the driver's seat. The Cardinal was shoved into the car's back seat. The man with the accent sat next to him, and the other gunman got in the front passenger seat to "ride shotgun." As the car pulled away from the monastery, the bells announcing the monks' early morning prayers began to toll. The masked gunmen had timed their abduction perfectly to avoid being discovered by sleepy monks on their way to the basilica for early morning prayers.

MATTINATA.

At 7 a.m., Father T celebrated Mass for the Cardinal's secretary and his housekeeper, in the residence's small chapel. He did not offer any reflections on the scripture readings at the time of the homily but, instead, suggested that they pray silently for the Cardinal and his safe return.

Afterward, the Sisters served him breakfast with American coffee, rolls, scrambled eggs and little sausages. The priest thanked his hosts profusely—reminding them that he had a lunch appointment that afternoon and, so, would not have lunch at the residence. They asked about his plans for supper, but he told them he wasn't sure what he would be doing that evening. He promised to let them know—one way or another—before he left for his afternoon appointment.

Just after nine o'clock, Father T walked through the front door of Interpol's Rome headquarters and asked to see the agent in charge. He didn't have to wait long before he was introduced to a man who identified himself as chief inspector, the head of the Rome office.

Father T explained that he was a priest from the United States whose family came from Sicily and that he had cousins just outside of Rome and in several small Sicilian towns. He told the chief inspector that he was a close friend of the Cardinal who had recently been threatened by terrorists and that the purpose of his visit was to learn more about this unfortunate situation and offer his assistance. He then produced the following letter from the commissioner of police in his hometown written on police department stationery, bearing the official seal of the city and witnessed by a notary public:

> To Whom It May Concern:
> Monsignor Salvatore E. Turiddu is a distinguished clergyman who has assisted our city's law enforcement agencies on numerous occasions. He is completely trustworthy and can offer insights and assistance not readily found elsewhere. For more information, please contact the undersigned or the agent in charge of our local office of the Federal Bureau of Investigation (FBI). Sincerely,
>
> ## W. R. Brindisi
> W. R. Brindisi
> Commissioner of Police

"*Bene. Bravissimo,*" the chief inspector said as he returned the letter to Father T. "It seems you have come just in time. We need all the help we can get—especially now."

"It will be my privilege to help in any way that I can, Inspector. The Cardinal is a good friend."

"I regret to inform you, *Monsignore,* that your friend the Cardinal was abducted last night from a small monastery in Umbria where he was staying after receiving several terrorist threats here in Rome and at the Vatican. Unfortunately I have no information to share with you except that he was seen being forced into a car by three masked men. A local woman on her way to work witnessed the abduction and alerted the *polizia* right away. Unfortunately, by the time the police arrived, the Cardinal and his abductors were long gone."

"This is insanity!" Father T said. "Where were his bodyguards? Where were the monks?"

"The two Interpol agents assigned to the Cardinal were drugged with a heavy sleep-inducing potion mixed with wine. They are being questioned now and will probably lose their jobs. It seems they accepted the bottle of wine as a gift from a young woman whose identity is unknown. The monks were all sleeping. The abduction happened in the early hours of the morning just before the monks were scheduled to say their morning prayers at 4 a.m. None of them saw or heard anything. If it hadn't been for the woman who saw the abduction and alerted the local *polizia*, it might have been several hours before anyone realized that your friend the Cardinal was missing."

"Jesus, Mary and Joseph, what a catastrophe!" exclaimed Father T. "So what are you doing to find the Cardinal and put these madmen out of business?"

"We're doing what we can, *Monsignore*, but unfortunately we don't have much to go on. We have no idea how the terrorists learned the Cardinal was in Norcia—or how they found the room he was given by the monks. Frankly, we hope that the terrorists will contact us soon and take responsibility for their actions. A ransom demand or some other "manifesto" from this group would at least give us some clue as to the kind of men we're dealing with. Then perhaps we can identify the source of their inside information."

"I was told this group calls itself The Sword of Justice. What information do you have about these terrorists? And what are you doing to apprehend their leaders?"

"Again, *Monsignore*, we are doing everything we can. Information about the so-called Sword of Justice is classified, and I am not permitted to discuss it with you, but I assure you we are taking this case very seriously."

"I certainly hope so," Father T said. "How do expect me to help you if you won't give me any information?"

"My apologies, *Monsignore*."

"Your agents are the ones whose unprofessional behavior caused this infuriating situation. Their actions were reprehensible, Chief Inspector, so I would think you would be especially motivated to find the Cardinal and ensure his safety!"

"I accept your criticism, *Monsignore*. Once again, I assure you that we are doing everything possible to make things right."

"This is insanity. Please keep me informed, Chief Inspector. I'm staying at the Cardinal's residence near the Vatican. Here is my cell-phone number while I'm in Italy," he said as he scribbled the number on a note pad on the chief inspector's desk. Please let me know if there's anything I can do."

"I will, *Monsignore*. I'm very sorry about your friend. I hope we will bring him back to you soon."

Father T's first impulse was to call his friend Msgr. Leone back home, but it was only 10 a.m. Rome time (3 a.m. back home). His friend was an early riser, but Father T decided to wait several hours before calling him. In the meantime, he went back to the Cardinal's residence and called his cousins who lived just outside the city. He knew they would be very disappointed if he didn't at least call them while in Rome on "official Church business." Father T was especially sensitive to his need to visit his cousins because he knew the eldest, Gioacchino, was seriously ill.

"No, I can't come for *cena* just yet," Father T told his cousins. "I will certainly come when my business is concluded here. Yes, I want to see you all, especially Gioacchino. I'll let you know as soon as I'm free. You can call my new cell phone—the number I just gave you—if you want to reach me here. Ciao Ciao."

It was obvious to Father T that the nuns who served as the Cardinal's secretary and housekeeper didn't know that His Eminence had been abducted. They went about their business and did not seem to be any more anxious than they were when he first arrived. The priest wrestled with his conscience, but in the end he decided not to tell them now but to wait until he had more information. The risk was that the Sisters would hear about it through the Vatican grapevine, or from a reporter calling for more information, but Father T chose to sin on the side of caution—at least until he was able to talk to his friend Msgr. Leone back home.

Sitting in the Cardinal's guest room, Father T attempted to read his breviary and say his morning prayers, but the most he was able to accomplish was an animated conversation with the Sacred Heart about the Cardinal's abduction.

"Sacred Heart of Jesus, have mercy on me, but I truly don't understand how you can allow these terrorist goons to kidnap the Cardinal. He's a good man, Lord, no matter what anyone says! He's dedicated his whole life to you,

Lord, so please don't let those bullies hurt him."

"And by the way, Lord, you know that I can't just stand by and let this happen without doing something about it. I've always been a man of action. I'm going to do whatever I can to find the Cardinal and make sure he comes home unharmed. Please, Lord, show me the way."

As he always did after he'd had his say, Father T forced himself to sit quietly and wait for the Sacred Heart to respond. He never saw visions, heard voices or witnessed miraculous changes in the weather. But he knew from experience that the Lord spoke to him—most often through the subtle promptings of his heart. If he talked too much, or was too impatient, there was a good chance he'd miss what the Sacred Heart was trying to tell him.

The Cardinal's residence was a remarkably quiet place considering the throngs of people, cars, buses and motorcycles just outside the building on the Via Conciliazione. Father T's mind wandered a bit, and before he knew it he was thinking of home—his parents and family, the priests he served with (especially his cousin Vince and his friends Bill, John and Mike) and the archbishop who had warned him before he left the United States: *You have to know the territory!*

"That's it!" Father T shouted to himself. "I have to find someone who knows the territory better than I do or I'll continue to be frustrated here!"

At home he had an extensive network of family, friends and coworkers who helped him whenever he was in a jam. For all of his 82 years, he counted on their help—and on the "street smarts" he developed growing up in the old neighborhood and, later, serving as an associate pastor and community organizer in the Italian neighborhood. Those street smarts had more than once earned him the title *il salvatore della città*, the savior of the city, and they were second nature to him—back home, perhaps, but not here in Rome!

Sure, he was an Italian-American who spoke the language fluently and who had visited Rome and Sicily nearly every year since his diaconate days, *but he didn't really know the territory!* Not the way a native would. Once he admitted that to himself, Father T was a new man. "I have to find someone who knows the territory better than I do or I'll never find the Cardinal and bring him home safely!"

Father T looked at the watch his brother Dominic had given him many years ago. It was almost 11 a.m. (5 a.m. back home). It was time to call his friend Bill who would certainly be awake now and getting ready to say his early morning Mass.

He dialed the number. "Bill, it's Sal. I'm calling from Rome. I'm sorry to call so early, but I have bad news. The Cardinal has been kidnapped by those terrorists! They drugged his bodyguards and then abducted him from a monastery somewhere—Norcia, I think they said it was. I've never been there, but they tell me it's an old Benedictine monastery in a small village in Umbria. That's all the information I have. I met with the Prefect of the Papal Household and with Interpol's chief inspector, but neither one of them was very helpful. I need someone who really knows the territory to help me track down these terrorists and bring the Cardinal home unharmed!"

Father T's friend was stunned. He knew the threats against the Cardinal were serious, but he never imagined the terrorists would succeed. It all seemed unreal, a nightmare that he hoped would end very soon!

"What can I do, Sal?"

"Get on the next flight over here. Seriously. I know it's a lot to ask, but I really need your help. The Cardinal's life may depend on it."

"Sal, you know I would do anything for the Cardinal, but are you sure I'm the right person? You said you need someone who knows the territory. I'm not a native. I'm an outsider like you. Besides, I'm older than you, and my health has not been great lately."

"Not true. You're healthy as a horse. And you know the Vatican inside and out. You have connections here that can help us cut through the bureaucracy and get the information we need to find the Cardinal. I need your help, Bill. You know I wouldn't ask you if I didn't."

"OK, Sal. Let me make a few phone calls and see what I can arrange. In the meantime, I'll make an appointment for you with the head of Vatican security. I hope that he can shed some more light on what happened in Norcia."

"You're a true friend, Bill. Thank you. I'll wait to hear from you later today."

"OK, Sal. Please take care of yourself. I'll see you soon—one way or another."

IL QUINTO GIORNO.
POMERIGGIO.
(Day Five. **Afternoon**)

The Cardinal was bound, gagged and blindfolded during the entire four-hour drive south from Norcia. His captors spoke only when necessary (in a language the Cardinal didn't understand), and they only stopped once—at a service plaza to purchase fuel, use the restroom and buy espresso and bottled water. They let the Cardinal go to the restroom—escorted by his captors after they had removed his gag, wrist restraints and blindfold—but they threatened to open fire on the rest stop's customers if he spoke or tried to get away.

During the brief period of time that he was not blind-folded, the Cardinal paid careful attention to the men who had abducted him. They were northern Europeans, not Italians, and they had rough, weathered faces and gruff mannerisms that showed they were used to getting their way. Only one of the men spoke to the Cardinal—in heavily accented English—which made him think that the others did not speak his language.

A couple of hours after they had resumed their trip (and the Cardinal was once again restrained, gagged and blindfolded), they arrived in what was clearly a large city. The Cardinal could hear the cars, buses and motor bikes as they moved slowly through the midday traffic. Based on the amount of time they had been on the road, and signs he had observed briefly at the service plaza, the Cardinal guessed he was in Naples—one of Italy's darkest, most dangerous and yet intriguing cities.

When the car stopped, the Cardinal's restraints were once again removed. The men did not wish to call attention to the man in simple priest's clothes whom they escorted through the narrow and crowded alleys of the densely populated city. The Cardinal had been to Naples before as a guest of the city's Cardinal Archbishop, but the guided tour he received from the archbishop's priest-secretary was limited to the Duomo (the cathedral), famous churches and museums, the *Teatro San Carlo* opera house, and some of the city's finer restaurants. He recalled the young priest saying that the back streets of Naples *are* the city's streets—with one or two arteries leading down to the port—but as his guide affirmed, the heart of Naples is its back alleys. That's why there are fewer tourists in Naples than in other Italian cities. They are afraid of pickpockets, muggers or worse. As a result, the tour buses bypass the city on their way to Pompeii and the Amalfi coast—or they discharge their passengers at the docks of the Bay of Naples where they boarded large ocean liners bound for Sicily or Greece and the Mediterranean islands.

As they walked, the Cardinal and his abductors passed small shops and *bassi* (small, single room homes) that were all filled to overflowing with *Napoletani* speaking their guttural dialect, gesturing broadly and arguing loudly about everything imaginable. The Cardinal spoke Italian very well, but his was a much more refined version of the *lingua Italiana*—the kind of Italian spoken by diplomats, academics and Vatican officials. What he heard coming from the doorways and back streets of Naples was a very different language, and it made him feel all the more isolated and afraid.

Finally, they arrived at their destination—a very old building that looked like it had once been a prison or some kind of armory. There were no windows—just thin slits at the top of the building almost to the rooftop that were originally designed to let in some sunlight but which now reflected only the permanent shadows of taller buildings. He found himself locked in a storage room with only a straw mattress and a chamber pot. It was a gloomy place that made his modest monk's cell in Norcia seem like a *palazzo*. Imprisoned and surrounded by darkness, the Cardinal's only recourse was to pray silently—and insistently—for the liberating light of Christ.

* * *

Father T began the afternoon by meeting the young seminarian, Michael O'Keefe, at the small ristorante called *Sor Eva* at the foot of the Janiculum Hill along the Tiber River. The young man was still wearing his black cassock. This would have irritated Father T back at home. (Priests of his generation didn't always understand why young seminarians, who grew up in a totally secularized culture, liked to wear the cassock as a symbol of their commitment to priestly studies.) But this was Rome, in proximity to the Vatican, and here Father T had reluctantly come to regard it as acceptable for clerics to wear their cassocks as if they were street clothes. Besides, he had more important things on his mind.

"What do you hear about the Cardinal?" Father T asked the seminarian.

"Just today we were told that he was abducted from the *Monastero di San Benedetto* in Norcia. The authorities believe a terrorist group is responsible, but there's been no official confirmation of that yet. We hear that the terrorist group The Sword of Justice is probably at work here. They hate the Catholic Church, and they've been looking for ways to hurt us. The Cardinal is one of their chief targets."

"Where are you getting your information?" Father T asked.

"Our rector is a good friend of the head of Vatican security. They speak frequently. Their conversations are supposed to be confidential, but there are no secrets in Vatican City. It's a wonder that the Cardinal's abduction isn't headline news around the world!"

"I have a feeling it will be soon," Father T thought to himself. "And I really need to act quickly before the media circus begins!"

The young seminarian and the senior pastor enjoyed their lunchtime conversation in spite of the circumstances and the fact that they were separated in age by nearly 60 years. Father T asked about the young man's family, and he told stories about the seminarian's home parish and the priests who served there long before Michael O'Keefe was born. The young man was fascinated. He had no idea his parish had such an interesting history.

"At one time, your parish sent more young men to the seminary than any other parish in the archdiocese," Father T said. "Msgr. Giannini, God rest his soul, was a pied piper of sorts. All the children—boys and girls— looked up to him, and they wanted to be like him. Each year, many young men from the parish entered the seminary, and an equal number of young women became nuns. Those were the days when priests could form close relationships with young people. It's a crying shame that all we ever hear about now are priests who have abused their sacred calling. So many more—the vast majority—are loyal and dedicated priests who are faithful to their vows and excellent role models for their young parishioners. Why don't we ever hear about them?"

"You're one of those faithful priests, Monsignor Turiddu. Everyone looks up to you."

"Not everyone, young man—believe me. But thank you for saying so. I've lived a long time, and I love being a priest. I hope you will too. Stay close to the Sacred Heart, and he won't let you down."

"Let me know if you hear anything more about the Cardinal," Father told his new friend. "Here's my cell phone number here in Italy—and my number back home. When you return to the States, come visit me at St. Roch. I'll prepare my Pasta Turiddu and veal spiedini. You'll think you're still in Italy!"

"Grazie, Monsignore. I hope you find a way to help the Cardinal."

"I will, Michael. If it's the last thing I do."

Father T returned to the Cardinal's residence with a heavy heart. He was frustrated by his lack of progress. "I just don't know the territory," he said. "When Bill gets here, things will be different. I just hope it's not too late."

The priest sat down in an easy chair in the Cardinal's guest room with the best of intentions of saying his prayers. He brought with him a prayer book compiled in the 1950s that he and his seminary classmates had used for their daily prayers. The pages were well-worn and the binding was very fragile now (more than 60 years later), but Father T took comfort in the old prayers—many of which he now knew by heart—and in the texture of the book itself which was so familiar to his sense of touch.

He didn't last long. Before he could finish the opening psalm, his head drooped and Father T was fast asleep.

As he slept, Father T dreamed that he was arguing with someone. Whoever it was spoke calmly and with authority, but the priest wasn't buying it.

"This is an absurdity! I'm going to stay here as long as it takes to find the Cardinal and bring him home. I've been a priest for more than 60 years, and I've never turned my back on a family member or friend in need. End of story."

"You're free to make your own decisions," the voice in Father T's dream said to him, "but it's dangerous here. I'm warning you: Go home where it's safe. You're too old for this."

"Nonsense!" Father T shouted so loudly that he woke himself up. The Cardinal's housekeeper heard him, too. She knocked softly on the guest room door.

"Is everything OK, Monsignor?"

"I'm fine, Sister. Just a bad dream."

"A nightmare," the priest muttered to himself. "Who was I talking to, and what does it mean?"

* * *

The Cardinal prayed quietly, but with greater intensity than he had ever prayed before. "Lord, I'm not a brave man. You know that. Give me courage to face whatever is coming. Give me strength to do your will."

Since being locked in the makeshift dungeon he now occupied, the Cardinal had seen no one and heard nothing except street noises. The slits near the ceiling that let in minimal light also allowed muffled sounds to make their way into his large, empty "cell." He had tried shouting, "*Aiutami. Sono un prigioniero!* (Help me. I'm a prisoner!)". But his words merely bounced off the armory's interior walls and seemed to go nowhere. The fact that his captors didn't come running as a result of his shouting led him to believe that he was either alone or unable to be heard.

"What do these men want from me?" the Cardinal asked himself. "I own nothing of value, and I certainly have no political power. What purpose does my abduction serve?"

Hours passed until nightfall. No one came to see him—or bring him food or water. The Cardinal began to fear that he had been brought to this place and then abandoned. He tried to prepare himself—mentally and spiritually—for a slow and painful death from starvation and dehydration.

Father T enjoyed a supper of risotto, veal piccata and salad prepared by the Sisters. Then he used the computer in the Cardinal's library to check his e-mail. His secretary had written out instructions for accessing the parish's e-mail account, and he followed them closely once he had logged onto the web using the directions provided by the Sisters when he first arrived.

There were more than 150 messages in Father T's inbox. Some were from friends and family passing along jokes or messages critical of politicians in Washington, D.C. Many were from various offices of the archdiocese. "In the old days, we used to get too much mail from the chancery," Father T used to say. "Now we get too much e-mail, too many faxes and even more street mail!"

Father T read down the list of messages looking for anything unusual. He nearly missed it because it was an unfamiliar username, but when he looked carefully he recognized a message from his friend John Vitale the retired police officer in Chicago.

After he clicked on the message, he read the following:

"Father, I tried calling the cell phone number you gave me, but it went right to voice mail. If you get this message, please call me. I have some information about The Sword of Justice. It's not much, but maybe it can help."

Father T looked at his watch. It was 8 p.m. in Rome (1 p.m. back home). He got his nonworking cell phone out of his bag and looked up his friend's telephone number stored in its address book. Then he used his new disposable phone to place the call. He reached his friend's voice mail and left a message. "This is Father. My cell phone doesn't work here so I picked up a new one. Here's the number: +39 347 893 0011. Please call me. Don't worry about the time difference. Call as soon as you can."

Father T's cell phone rang almost immediately, but it wasn't his friend from Chicago. It was Msgr. Leone calling to tell him he would arrive at 7 the next morning on the same Alitalia flight Father T had taken two days earlier.

"A Vatican driver will meet me and bring me to the Cardinal's residence," his friend told him. "We should be there before 9."

"You're a good friend, Bill—to the Cardinal and to me. Thank you!"

"It's not a problem, Sal. Truth be told, once I found out that the Cardinal had been kidnapped, wild horses couldn't have kept me away!"

"Get some rest tonight, Sal. We'll have a busy day tomorrow. The head of Vatican security will see us at noon."

"I hope we have better luck than I did yesterday. All smiles but no substance!"

"Things have changed now that the Cardinal has been kidnapped," Msgr. Leone said. "The Vatican is desperate now."

"Well, I'm desperate, too. I've been here two days with nothing to show for it."

"Be patient, Sal. As you always say, the Sacred Heart has everything under control."

"Thank you, my friend. *Buon viaggio!*"

* * *

It was just after 10 p.m. when the Cardinal heard someone insert a key in the door. The room was pitch black with no light since nightfall. The large, rough-looking man who entered carried a lantern and a tray with a bottle of water, a small loaf of bread and some cheese.

"I've brought your dinner," the man said. It was the same man who had abducted him—the only one who had spoken. "We need to keep you strong for tomorrow's interrogation."

"Interrogation?" The Cardinal was genuinely surprised. "What could you possibly hope to learn from me? I have no secrets to disclose even if you torture me."

"Oh, we don't want to learn any secrets from you, sir. We only want your undivided attention."

"You could have gotten my attention without kidnapping me and locking me up in this horrible place," the Cardinal said."

"Not likely, sir. You're not known for your listening skills—or for your willingness to consider other points of view."

"Try me," said the Cardinal.

"Don't worry, sir. We will."

The large man left the tray and the lantern and headed for the door. As he left, the Cardinal heard him say something to someone in the outer room, but since he didn't understand the language, it didn't mean anything to him.

IL SESTO GIORNO.
MATTINATA.
(Day Six. Morning)

Father T said the early morning Mass for the Sisters, but before the opening prayer he told them that the Cardinal had been kidnapped. He decided he couldn't wait any longer. It wasn't fair to them, and he was counting on their prayers to help ensure the Cardinal's safety.

"The Cardinal is following in our Lord's footsteps," Father T said during his brief homily. "He was also abducted by hoodlums and taken away like a common criminal. Let's pray that our Lord's example will inspire the Cardinal and help him endure the indignities he is surely experiencing at the hands of these thugs!"

After Mass, the Sisters served a modest Italian-style *prima colazione* (breakfast) of coffee and rolls. They offered to prepare eggs and sausages, but Father T declined. He knew they all had a lot on their minds. (Try as they might, they couldn't hide the tears that continued to moisten their eyes. Nor could they suppress the involuntary sighs that came frequently as they went about their daily chores.)

"Father, thank you for being here to comfort and encourage us," the Cardinal's secretary said. "I don't know what we would do without you."

"I'm honored to be here," Father T said. "And I promise you, even if it's the last thing I do, the Cardinal will be home soon!"

Shortly before 9 a.m., Msgr. Leone arrived. Father T was relieved to see him, and so were the Sisters.

"How was your flight, Bill? Any problems?"

"No, Sal. It just seemed longer than usual—I guess I'm impatient because of the circumstances."

"I know how you feel. Time is running out. We need to find the Cardinal and bring him home!"

"You're right, Sal, but where do we start?"

"We start with The Sword of Justice. Who are these people, and what do they want? If we can only get some kind of break here—and learn more about the thugs who kidnapped the Cardinal—there's a good chance we can find him and set him free."

Just then, Father T's cell phone began to vibrate in his shirt pocket. When he looked at the caller ID, he saw that it was his niece Anna calling from home. Knowing it was the middle of the night back home, he immediately thought of his sisters.

"Yes, Anna. What's up? Why are you calling me at this hour? How are Aunt Jenny and Aunt Anne?"

"They're fine, Uncle Sal. That's not why I'm calling. Your friend John Vitale in Chicago has been trying to get a hold of you. He says it's urgent. I gave him this number, but for some reason, he can't get through. I told him I would try. Please call him now."

"I will Anna. You go back to bed. I'm sorry you had to be disturbed."

"If taking a call in the middle of the night helps bring the Cardinal home safely, it's the least I can do. Please be careful, Uncle Sal."

"I will, Anna. Msgr. Leone is here with me now. At noon we're going to see the head of Vatican security."

"Call John Vitale first. He sounds pretty agitated."

"I'll place the call as soon as we hang up."

"Ciao, Uncle Sal."

John Vitale had retired from the Chicago Police Department after 35 years of faithful service. He was a good cop—honest, tough as nails, but dedicated to community service. He first met Father T at a meeting of the Italian-American Society in Chicago in the 1970s when the priest was fully engaged as an associate pastor, an urban planner and an active member of the Italian-American Society. The rookie policeman didn't quite know how to take the activist priest. In those days, Father T had long, jet-black hair and a mustache. His mother couldn't stand the long hair. (She made him wear a hairnet in her kitchen!) And the seminary wouldn't let him teach his class on urban affairs as long as he had facial hair, which was against the rules for the seminary's students and faculty. (Father T shaved the mustache, but he had his neighborhood barber make a false one using his own hair. When his weekly class at the seminary was finished, he wore the false mustache as a sign of his independence!)

"Giovanni, this is Father. I know it's early, but my niece Anna said it was urgent. What do you have for me?"

"An undercover agent in the Chicago Police Department has been attending meetings of the local chapter of The Sword of Justice. He says the group is definitely responsible for kidnapping the Cardinal."

"Do you know where they've taken him?" Father T asked. "We really need to find him, Giovanni."

"We don't know the location yet, but our guy is working on it. He has to be careful not to blow his cover. He says that CPD is notifying Interpol. I'll call you when I know more. Can you give me your Italian cell phone number again? I don't think I have the right number."

Father T repeated the number.

"Anything else you can tell me, Giovanni?"

"All we know is that The Sword of Justice is planning some kind of big anti-Catholic demonstration. They hope to embarrass the Church by making a fool of the Cardinal—getting him to make outrageous statements that will discredit him and the Vatican in the eyes of the world. Unfortunately, right now we have no idea when, or how, all this is supposed to happen."

"You're a good friend, Giovanni. Please stay in touch."

"God bless you, Father, and please be safe. These guys can be nasty."

"I grew up in the same kind of neighborhood you did, Giovanni. We know how to handle "nasty" goons like these guys! My best to your wife and family. God bless you!"

Msgr. Leone had reserved a guest room at the North American College. When Father T said that his friend Bill "knew the territory," he was referring to the nearly ten years he lived and worked in Rome and to the strong relationships he formed with Vatican officials in the various departments of the Roman Curia, including the Secretariat of State, congregations, tribunals, councils and offices, especially the Apostolic Camera, the Administration of the Patrimony of the Apostolic See and the Prefecture for the Economic Affairs of the Holy See. The Vatican bureaucracy was a world that Father T couldn't begin to comprehend, but with Msgr. Leone at his side he felt a new confidence. Together, they knew the territory.

Vatican security is the responsibility of the Corps of Gendarmerie of the Vatican City State. It is not to be confused with the colorful Swiss Guards whose sole duty is to protect the pope. The corps functions as the Vatican's police force. Approximately 130 highly trained law enforcement professionals serve as security for the small city state. They also ensure public order, safety, and border and traffic control. The corps investigates crimes that are committed within its jurisdiction. They also staff the Vatican Fire Brigade!

Father T was eager to meet with the man in charge. He was desperate to find the Cardinal and bring him home safely.

IL SESTO GIORNO.
MEZZO GIORNO.
(Day Six. Noon)

Father T and Msgr. Leone were scheduled to meet with the inspector general, the head of the Vatican's Corps of Gendarmerie, at noontime. Msgr. Leone knew him fairly well because he began his term with the gendarmerie around the same time that Msgr. Leone began his assignment as a spiritual director for seminarians at the North American College.

"Benvenuto, caro Monsignore Leone. E' sempre un piacere vederti." The inspector general spoke in Italian and extended his arms to welcome him as an old friend and let him know how glad he was to see him again..

"Inspector General, it is my privilege to introduce one of our archdiocese's most distinguished clergymen, and my good friend, Monsignor Salvatore Turiddu. We are deeply grateful for your taking the time to meet with us. We know how busy you are—especially now."

"Welcome, *Monsignore* Turiddu. Your reputation precedes you. We are honored to have your assistance in this most difficult and perplexing business involving one of the Holy See's most important persons, the head of the Apostolic Signatura, our Supreme Court."

"The Cardinal is a dear friend to Msgr. Leone and me, Inspector," Father T said. "We will let nothing stand in the way of his safety and his immediate return to his ministry here in the Vatican. Please let us know how we can assist you."

"Unfortunately, we still have very little information to share with you," said the inspector general. The Sword of Justice appears to be responsible for the Cardinal's abduction, but no one has yet taken responsibility for his kidnapping and the evidence is entirely circumstantial. In fact, it's only by hearsay and process of elimination that we can identify The Sword of Justice as the perpetrators of this heinous crime."

"Inspector, a friend of mine in Chicago, a retired police officer, tells me that a reliable source confirms that The Sword of Justice is responsible. He says these thugs are planning some kind of anti-Catholic campaign, and they want to use the Cardinal to somehow discredit the Church. They don't know him very well if they think he would ever betray his faith."

"We have heard these rumors, too, *Monsignore*, but so far we have no concrete evidence."

"Have you infiltrated The Sword of Justice's cell here in Rome?" Msgr. Leone asked. "I understand there are groups that meet in every major city of Europe and North America. Surely they have a presence here in Rome."

"The Corps of Gendarmerie of the Vatican City State has no undercover agents," the inspector general replied. "As you undoubtedly know from your many years in residence here, we are understaffed due to budget cuts. We must rely on Interpol, the Carabinieri and the *Polizia di Roma* for this kind of work. I know they are doing their best, but it is very frustrating for us to be so restricted in our efforts to protect one of our very own."

"If you did have the necessary resources, Inspector General, what would you do that is not being done now?" asked Father T. "Perhaps we can help."

"What is needed most is access to the Rome group, the terrorist cell that is closest to us here but so far inaccessible. But it would take months for a trained operative to gain the trust of the members. As you know, they are virulently anti-Catholic and anti-Vatican. I doubt that any of us would stand a chance trying to break-in to their inner circle."

"If that's what it takes to free the Cardinal," Father T said, "Msgr. Leone and I are certainly willing to give it a try, Inspector. Can you at least point us in the right direction? We need to know where their headquarters are and when they meet. We'll figure it out from there."

"I shouldn't encourage you," the inspector general said. "We could be starting an international incident. But as I said earlier, you're reputation as *il salvatore della città* precedes you, *Monsignore*. That's why I'm willing to give this a try—as crazy as it seems. I also have confidence in your friend Msgr. Leone. His advice is always sound and balanced. I'm sure he will keep you from doing something we'll all regret."

"I'm not sure I share your confidence in me," Msgr. Leone said, "but I appreciate it. You can be sure that I will do everything in my power to ensure that Monsignor Turiddu and our friend the Cardinal are safe."

"We're grateful for your time this afternoon, Inspector General," said Father T. Please let us know when you will be able to brief us on the Roman group of The Sword of Justice. We're eager to get started in our quest to find the

Cardinal and bring him home safely."

"We've learned that all members of the Rome group of The Sword of Justice have been asked to attend a special meeting this evening. We think it may be possible for you to infiltrate this meeting. Why don't you meet me back here at 1600 hours—after the afternoon break? That will give my staff time to brief you on the details of tonight's meeting and outline a strategy for getting you inside. May the Madonna guide us! It will not be easy to do this, but perhaps with her help we can find a way."

"*Mille grazie*, Inspector," Msgr. Leone said. "We are deeply grateful. We will return here at 1600 hours."

IL SESTO GIORNO.
POMERIGGIO.
(Day Six. Afternoon)

Father T and Msgr. Leone returned to the Cardinal's residence where the Sisters served them "a light lunch." The lunch may have been light by Italian standards, but it was certainly not what the two Americans were used to. The Sisters served homemade soup, pasta with vodka sauce, veal medallions and steamed vegetables. The desserts they offered (assorted sweets, or as the Italians say, *dolci*) were declined politely but firmly by the two guests.

"Basta, grazie," Father T said. "Thank you, but we've had enough. We can't possibly eat any more!"

Msgr. Leone returned to the NAC to unpack his suitcase and rest up from the long flight. Father T sat down in the guest room to say midday prayers. Neither got much rest during the afternoon siesta. Their minds were on The Sword of Justice and the briefing that they would receive later that afternoon.

Father T had just nodded off in his easy chair when his cell phone rang.

"Pronto," he answered. *"Chi parla?"*

"It's me," Msgr. Cugino said. "How are you? Did Bill Leone arrive safely?"

"Yes, Vinnie. Bill and I met with the head of Vatican security a couple of hours ago. He's going to help us track down the thugs who belong to the local chapter of The

Sword of Justice. We need to find the Cardinal and bring him home safely."

"Are you planning to go there by yourselves or will you have law enforcement officers with you?"

"We're playing this by ear, Vinnie. We won't know what our strategy is until we meet with the inspector general and members of his staff later today."

"Well, stay close to them, Sal. Even with Bill's help, you're still a foreigner in a strange land. You don't know what kind of trouble you might get yourself into if you and Msgr. Leone try to infiltrate The Sword of Justice without professional help. You're both in your 80s, for Christ's sake. Please don't do anything foolish"

"I wouldn't exactly call myself *uno straniero* (a foreigner), Father. (He called his cousin "Father" when he was irritated with him.) I've been to Rome so many times that I know the city like the back of my hand. I can take care of myself. So can Bill. It's true that we're not as young as we used to be, but we're both in good health. We'll be fine."

"OK, Sal. I'll back off. Just be careful. Please."

"I will be careful, Vinnie. I promise. The Sacred Heart is with me. He's never let me down yet. Besides, I do have friends and family here. They won't let me down either. I'll let you know how it goes."

"That's all I ask, Sal. God be with you."

"Thank you, Vincenzo. *Ciao!*"

Father T's brief conversation with his cousin Vinnie had given him an idea. He immediately called the North American College and asked to speak to his new seminarian friend, Michael O'Keefe. After speaking with his young friend, he placed another call—this time to his cousins who lived just outside of Rome and spoke with the eldest, Gioacchino.

"Well, that should make Vinnie happy," the priest said to himself. "We now have a backup plan!"

* * *

Father T walked the short distance to the Vatican. On his way, he encountered beggars on every corner. He couldn't bring himself to pass without tossing some small coins in the cups or baskets held out to him by the city's poor. "I've been blessed all these years," he said to himself. "Now it's payback time."

Msgr. Leone was waiting on the street outside the front door of the Missionaries of Charity headquarters in Rome. Together they walked to the Vatican entrance closest to the inspector general's office. Two Swiss Guards saluted as Msgr. Leone presented his credentials and escorted Father T, who was wearing his best cassock and purple sash, into the courtyard just outside the Paul VI Audience Hall.

"What's our strategy, Sal?"

"As I told Vinnie when he called earlier, we're playing this by ear. I'm afraid he wasn't very happy with me. He wants us to stick close to the *polizia* and not take any risks."

"Msgr. Cugino is just concerned for our safety."

"I know, Bill. I was too short with him, but I really do think we know how to handle ourselves—even if we are in our 80s and 5,000 miles from home!"

The inspector general welcomed them back to his office. Two other men were with him—the chief inspector of Interpol's Rome office and the Prefect of the Papal

Household.

"I'm well-acquainted with these gentlemen," Father T said as the head of Vatican security introduced them to the two Americans. "I hope you have better information for us than you did when we met earlier!"

Msgr. Leone was very familiar with Prefect of the Papal Household, but he did not know the Interpol agent.

"We're here in Rome to cooperate with you and assist you in any way possible. Please tell us how we can help," Father T's friend said.

"As we discussed earlier today, we need someone to infiltrate the local chapter of The Sword of Justice," the inspector general said. "We don't expect that these terrorists will allow you into their inner circle, but there is an outside chance that you can engage them in conversation and pick up some valuable information in the process. At this point, any leads no matter how slim will be an improvement on our current situation."

"How do we go about engaging these thugs in conversation?" Father T asked.

"We have reliable information that the Rome chapter is meeting this evening in one of Rome's most popular restaurants on the *Via Veneto*," the chief inspector of Interpol said. It's a long shot, but we think we can get you into the private room accidentally as American tourists who have lost their way. Once you're inside, you're on your own, but we'll be listening to your conversation, and if anything goes wrong, we'll break down the doors, if necessary, to protect you from any harm."

"Why does this sound like *déjà vu* all over again?" Father T said. "I've been here before—back home! I can't speak for Msgr. Leone but I'm willing to give this a try, but the accidental tourist bit seems pretty far-fetched especially for two elderly priests."

"You know I'm with you, Sal," Msgr. Leone said. "It's so far-fetched that it just might work!"

"Are you both willing to wear recording devices?" the Interpol agent asked.

"Yes," Father T said. "Based on my previous experience, if I turned you down you'd only find another way to bug the restaurant and record the conversation anyway."

"That's right, *Monsignore*. One way or another we must record your conversation," the inspector general said. "The best way to accomplish that is for you and Msgr. Leone to wear recording devices."

"Once we are in the private room where The Sword of Justice's Rome members are meeting, what's our strategy?" Msgr. Leone asked. "Do we just go up to the head honcho and ask him where the heck the Cardinal is?"

"Excuse me, but what does the expression 'head honcho' mean?" the papal prefect asked.

"I'm sorry, Your Excellency," Msgr. Leone said. "It means the man in charge."

"*Ohimè, grazie!*" the prefect said. "I should have known."

"That will be up to you and Father T," the Interpol agent said. "I would start with polite conversation and go from there. In the end, a direct question might get you more information than you think."

"OK. Let's get started then. We didn't come all the way to Rome to chitchat with terrorists," said Father T, "but if that's what it takes to find our Cardinal, that's what we're going to do!"

"Where do we meet you this evening and what time?" Msgr. Leone asked.

"The lobby of the Hotel Grand Flora on the *Via Veneto* at 2000 hours," the Interpol agent said. "The restaurant is just a block away. Dress like American tourists."

"I'll borrow a pair of blue jeans and a flower shirt from one of the seminarians," Msgr. Leone said. "Father T can wear his sweater and everyday slacks."

"We'll blend right in with the *fashionistas* on the Via Veneto!" Father T said.

The inspector general thanked them both for their willingness to help gather valuable information that he hoped would lead to the Cardinal's whereabouts.

"That's what we do," Father T said. "We do whatever it takes to help our friends. End of conversation!"

The two friends walked back to the Cardinal's residence past the Swiss Guards, through the Bernini columns and across St. Peter's Square. Pilgrims from all over the world were lined up on the opposite side of the *piazza* waiting to pass through the security screens so that they could enter the world's most famous church—St. Peter's Basilica.

Father T thought back to his first time here. Following his diaconate ordination, the young Sicilian-American and a classmate journeyed to Europe on a ship that sailed from Canada to England. Although it was June, the weather was so cold that Father T and his friend were on deck only twice—the day they sailed and they day they arrived! After spending a few days in England, they crossed the English Channel by ferry and landed in France where they rented a car.

"We drove that car right up to those steps," Father T

was pointing at the marble steps leading up to the front doors of St. Peter's Basilica. "No car can do that now unless it's a popemobile!"

"My friend Charlie was with me," the priest said. "He died too young, and I miss him every day. But I'm grateful for old friends like you, Bill. I know you didn't have to come all the way over here, but I'm very glad you did."

"You said it yourself, Sal. We do whatever it takes to help our friends."

When they arrived at the Cardinal's residence, Msgr. Leone logged onto the computer in the library to check his e-mail messages. Father T said his evening prayers. Since he wasn't sure what time they would return from The Sword of Justice meeting, he thought he would pray now, asking the Sacred Heart for his special protection in the coming hours.

IL SESTO GIORNO.
SERA.
(Day Six. Evening)

The Cardinal was very uncomfortable in his make-shift prison in Naples. His hands and feet were still sore from the plastic strips that had tightly bound them during the long trip from Norcia to Napoli, and he had been sitting on the straw mattress on the cold floor for many hours. His captors fed him bread and cheese with water to drink. When nature called, he used the chamber pot, which thankfully they emptied whenever it was full. All in all, it was a horrible experience—unlike anything the Cardinal had ever known. He prayed fervently for courage and for the strength to endure whatever was to come. Not knowing was the hardest part. What were these brutal men planning? The Cardinal feared the worst.

Father T and Msgr. Leone took a taxi to the *Via Veneto*—Rome's fashion district, the favorite gathering place of the rich and famous. The Hotel Grand Flora, which is located just outside the old city wall across from the famous *Villa Borghese* gardens, was once a private residence (*un pala-zzo*). It was commandeered by the Nazis during World War II and used as officers' quarters. Now it was a home in Rome for "glitterati" and for wealthy business people from all over the world.

Interpol's chief inspector was waiting for them in the lobby along with two technicians who would wire them for sound. The inspector guided them into a parlor located off the lobby, and the technicians went to work.

"Wearing a wire used to be very cumbersome and unreliable," the inspector said. "Modern listening devices are simpler and much more effective. You can forget you're wearing them. Just engage in normal conversation. I promise we'll hear every word that is said, and we'll know exactly where you are at all times."

"That's a comfort," Msgr. Leone said. "But shouldn't we have some kind of code word to alert you when something is going wrong?"

"It's not necessary," the Interpol inspector said. "But if it makes you feel more secure, let's choose one."

"Jesus, Mary and Joseph!" Father T said.

The others looked at him expecting something more.

"That's the code," the priest explained. "If you hear either one of us say 'Jesus, Mary and Joseph,' please come running."

"Jesus, Mary and Joseph!" Msgr. Leone repeated. "I like it, but I hope I never have to say it."

"It's time to go, gentlemen. We can't go with you, but I promise you we'll be close by at all times. Just cross the street to the restaurant called 'Harry's Bar.' When you get inside, go to the bar and sit down. In a few minutes, a waiter (an undercover Interpol agent) will escort you to the private room where members of The Sword of Justice are meeting. He'll enter the room with a tray of drinks, and you follow him. Act like tourists who've gone through the wrong door by mistake, and begin engaging the members in conversation. From there you're on your own."

"What are the chances these guys will say anything to

us that's helpful?" Msgr. Leone asked.

"Very slim," the chief inspector said. "But stranger things have happened. Besides, we're going to give you each an additional listening device to leave behind when you leave. The room will be carefully 'swept' just prior to the meeting, so we couldn't plant a bug ahead of time. But it's quite possible that a listening device you bring with you into the room, and then leave there, will not be detected. It's worth a shot," he said, "if you're willing to give it a try."

"I'm not worried," Father T said. "The Sacred Heart will guide us. We're going to find the Cardinal. End of story."

In Rome, Harry's Bar is something of a legend. The café has been in existence since 1918, but the current restaurant and bar with its American theme was established in 1959 during the golden age of Fellini's *La Dolce Vita* and the days when Frank Sinatra sang at the piano and a dazzling array of American and European film stars frequented "the exclusive and fascinating Harry's Bar."

Still boasting a rich and famous clientele, Harry's Bar seemed an odd place for a clandestine meeting of The Sword of Justice. Journalists and paparazzi were everywhere waiting to sight some unsuspecting star caught in the act of cheating on his or her spouse or "partner" and soon to be the front-page story of all the tabloids. It was either an act of extreme hubris or a carefully designed strategy for a group of left-wing terrorists to gather in one of the most "open" and visible places in the city of Rome!

Needless to say, in all his 38 trips to Rome since the mid-1950s, Father T had never been to Harry's Bar. This was definitely not his kind of place. In fact, as he and Msgr. Leone walked in the door, they both felt very much out of place.

Following the chief inspector's instructions, they went straight to the bar and ordered drinks. Father T had Campari with soda (he found that the soda softened the bitterness of the traditional Italian *aperitif*). Msgr. Leone asked for some white wine and was given a Frascati (a dry, light-bodied wine from the Frascati area south of Rome). The two Americans attempted to chitchat while they waited, but under the circumstances making "small talk" was the last thing either wanted to do. The chief inspector cautioned them to only speak English in order to reinforce their "cover" as American tourists, so they resisted the temptation to order their drinks, or act like they understood what was said to them, in Italian.

After about 10 minutes waiting, one of the servers approached them and said in English, "Please come with me, and bring your drinks with you." He was carrying a tray of drinks, and he led them across the restaurant to a private room whose double doors were closed.

"Follow me, but don't say anything until you get inside and someone asks what you're doing there. Then act like you're lost. When you leave, don't forget to leave your drink glasses in the room on one of the side tables. We have planted listening devices in your glasses' false bottoms."

The two Americans did as they were told. The undercover agent opened one of the double doors and entered the room. Father T and Msgr. Leone followed carrying their drinks with them.

It was an elegant room with its *boiserie*, an ornate and intricately carved style of wood paneling, and its fine bas-relief plasters. At the far end of the room was a head table and podium that seated six men including an impeccably well-dressed man with a full head of flowing white hair who was speaking. About 30 men sat at round tables of 5 each. All were listening intently to the speaker who addressed them in Italian but with an accent that suggested he was not a native.

The men had their backs to the American intruders and did not appear to notice them at first. The speaker was so engrossed in what he was saying that he didn't pay any attention to them either. This brief period of invisibility allowed Father T and Msgr. Leone to quietly place their "bugged" glasses on a serving table near the main doors. It also gave them a chance to listen to what the speaker was saying.

"For 2,000 years now, the Catholic church has systematically robbed us Europeans of our freedom, our culture and our religious roots. It is time for us to forcibly reject the Christian heresy and return to the secular paganism that was the glory of ancient Rome and that inspired all the native European peoples who inhabited this great continent prior to the Christian invasions."

"Huh?" Father T thought to himself but didn't dare say. "Secular paganism? Give me a break!"

"We plan to expose the church's hypocrisy once and for all," the speaker continued. "We now have in our custody one of the highest ranking officials in the Vatican. Within a matter of days, his signed confession will be published on the Internet and in every newspaper and television program across the globe. He will confess to all the unspeakable crimes that have been committed by evil popes and bishops for the past 2,000 years. Victory will be ours, and the great whore that is the Roman church will be revealed for what it is—once and for all!"

"*Basta! Quest'è una sciocchezza!*" Father T shouted in Italian. "Enough of this insanity. I will not permit you to blaspheme Holy Mother Church, the Body of Christ. Shame on you for what you have said—and more importantly for what you have done to our Cardinal, a good man and a faithful son of the Church!"

Every eye in the room turned to see who was speaking. Two large men (Father T would later call them "thugs") raced to the back of the room, grabbed the two Americans and began to push them toward a door that led to an alley behind the restaurant.

"Wait," said the speaker. "Since they have chosen to eavesdrop on our meeting let them hear what I have to say in conclusion. Obviously it concerns them greatly."

"We've heard enough," said Msgr. Leone speaking in English and hoping to do some damage control. "We're from America, and we got into this room by mistake. We're Catholic priests and my friend here was startled to hear you speak negatively about our Church. We mean you no harm. Please just let us go."

"I'd be prepared to believe you, sir, except that your outspoken friend referenced 'our cardinal.' How is it that two innocent American priests such as yourselves know that one of your cardinals is missing and, in fact, is a prisoner of The Sword of Justice?"

"We heard rumors," Father T said. "It doesn't take a genius to guess that the missing Cardinal we heard about earlier today is the high ranking Vatican official you said you had in custody."

"Perhaps. But we're not taking any chances. Remove the two Americans. We'll take them with us to Napoli where they will join their precious cardinal and witness his ignominy."

The two thugs escorted their prisoners out the exit door to the alley where they bound their hands and feet and forced them into the same black SUV that had transported the Cardinal from the monastery in Norcia to his confinement in Naples.

All this time, Interpol was listening, waiting for the prearranged signal ("Jesus, Mary and Joseph!"), but the two Americans never gave it. The chief inspector resisted the urge to rescue the two Americans anyway. He was hoping that they would still be able to learn something about the Cardinal's whereabouts. Once the speaker said that Father T and Msgr. Leone would be taken to Naples to join the Cardinal, he decided that the best course was to wait and hope that The Sword of Justice would take them unharmed to the place where the Cardinal was being held. It was a risk, but he persuaded himself that since they didn't give the signal the two Americans would agree it was the only choice they had if they wanted to rescue the Cardinal.

From where the Interpol agents were located, they could not see where Father T and Msgr. Leone were taken once they were escorted out of the room into the street behind Harry's Bar. But, fortunately, the wires planted on them by Interpol also functioned as GPS tracking devices. A car with two Interpol agents was quickly dispatched to identify the SUV and follow it all the way to Naples where they would be met by a team of local agents. Meanwhile the chief inspector and his two technicians remained behind and listened to what the speaker had to say "in conclusion" to The Sword of Justice members gathered in Harry's back room.

"Soon we will go public with the cardinal's confession and with our plans to discredit the Roman church. That will be a triumphant day for our movement! We will show the world how corrupt Christianity is and why it has no place in the future of Europe or the world as we envision it!"

"How will we accomplish this?" one of the members asked. "Surely we will be accused of international terrorism if we continue to kidnap church officials and their American friends."

"The world will see that our actions are justified. Once the media get hold of this story they will downplay the means we have employed and instead focus all the world's attention on the church's hypocrisy. I can assure you, our Catholic enemies will be damaged irreparably, and The Sword of Justice will emerge unscathed!"

The speaker invited all the members present to rise and recite an oath of allegiance to their brotherhood. When they were finished, the speaker informed the group that he was leaving for *Napoli* by private jet to interrogate the Cardinal and secure his confession. He promised that it was only a matter of days before victory was assured.

The chief inspector rushed from the room to his waiting car. He instructed the driver to take him to Interpol's headquarters where a helicopter was waiting to transport him to a private airfield. He was determined to arrive in

Naples before the speaker and long before the SUV carrying Father T and his old friend.

* * *

Back home, Father T's niece Anna was on the telephone talking to Father Mike.

"I haven't heard from Uncle Sal since yesterday. It's after 9 p.m. Rome time, and he hasn't called anyone—you, Father Vince, Father John or anyone at St. Roch. And he doesn't answer the cell phone he picked up over there. Don't you think that's strange?"

"Yes, Anna," Father Mike said. "It's not like Sal to be out of touch for a whole day. I know that he and Bill were supposed to meet with the head of Vatican security this afternoon. Why don't I make some calls and see if I can find out anything."

"Thank you, Father. I'll call Msgr. Leone's sister Clare and see if she's heard from her brother."

"OK, but don't worry her unnecessarily. Just because we haven't heard from Sal doesn't mean there's anything wrong."

"I know. I'll be very casual, and I'll let you know what she says. Call me as soon as you hear something."

"I will, Anna," Father Mike said. "You'll be the first to know whatever I know."

Anna reached Msgr. Leone's sister Clare immediately.

"Hi, Clare. I'm Anna Dominica, Father T's niece. We met a couple of years ago at my Uncle Sal's 80th birthday party."

"I remember you," Clare said. "What a wonderful party. The Osteria really outdid itself that night!"

"With frozen custard 'imported' from south city's best outdoor ice cream stand!"

"How can I help you, Anna?"

"I was just wondering if you've heard from Msgr. Leone since he arrived in Rome. Uncle Sal usually calls once a day, but we haven't heard from him today. He probably got distracted by all his meetings at the Vatican, but it's not like him to go a whole day without checking in."

"Bill called me early this morning (our time) to let me know he arrived safely. He said that he and Father T met with the head of Vatican security. I haven't heard anything since then."

"If you hear from him, will you ask him if Uncle Sal is OK? I'm probably overreacting, but my uncle is 82 years old and he doesn't always use the best judgment. Last year, he climbed out a window on the 14th floor of a building at 8th and Carr to escape from terrorists who were holding him hostage. If the police SWAT team hadn't been on the roof ready to rescue him, there's no telling what might have happened to him."

"Don't worry, Anna," Clare said. "I'm sure Father T is OK, but I'll let you know as soon as I hear from my brother."

Father Mike was not as successful. His calls to the Vatican and to the North American College went to voicemail, and he could only hope (and pray) that they would be returned. He then called the Cardinal's residence and spoke to the Sister who served as the Cardinal's secretary. She told him that Father T and Msgr. Leone had lunch at the Cardinal's residence and then met with the Vatican's head of security. They did not have supper at the residence that night, but she said that around seven o'clock Rome time Father T had asked her to call for a taxi to the Hotel Grand Flora on the Via Veneto. That was now more than three hours ago, and she had not heard anything from him since then although it was getting late. (Father T was rarely out past 10 p.m., she told Father Mike, but she reminded him that full course dinners in Rome—especially on the Via Veneto—can be rather lengthy depending on the occasion or the company.)

Father Mike apologized a second time for calling so late, and he thanked Sister for her help.

"I'm sure this will be unnecessary," he said, "but will you please let me know if he's still not there when you attend your morning Mass? Please call me anytime—day or night."

"*Santi numi!*" Sister exclaimed. "I can't imagine Father T staying out all night without calling us. For one thing, he's supposed to say Mass for us tomorrow. Surely he'll call and let us know if he can't make it."

"I'm sure he will, Sister. I don't mean to worry you, but as you know some very bad men have the Cardinal in their custody, and everyone who is close to him needs to be very careful right now. I'm just double-checking to make sure that Father T and Msgr. Leone are OK."

"I know, Father. God bless the Cardinal—and all of us!"

IL SESTO GIORNO.
NOTTE.
(Day Six. Late Night)

The impeccably well-dressed, white-haired man who spoke to The Sword of Justice members in Rome was known as the Grand Inquisitor of the Order. He was the mastermind for all Sword of Justice activities. Intelligent, polished and deadly serious even when he smiled and oozed charm from every pore, the inquisitor was used to getting his way. He detested priests above all human beings, and the higher the rank (monsignor, bishop, cardinal or pope), the more he despised and ridiculed them behind their backs.

"Bring the cardinal to me," he demanded shortly after his arrival in Naples. "I want to interrogate him and secure his confession. Time is running out."

The man who served as the Cardinal's prison guard once again bound his hands with plastic strips and then brought the exhausted and frightened prelate to a room that had once served as an office in the abandoned armory building. The grand inquisitor was standing behind an old wooden desk. He motioned for the Cardinal to be seated in a straightbacked chair in the center of the room.

"Good evening, sir," said the inquisitor with a feigned courtesy that the Cardinal recognized for exactly what it was: hostility in disguise. "I'm pleased to have this opportunity to tell you why you are here. I also have some very important questions to ask you."

"I'll be happy to answer any questions to the best of my ability," the Cardinal said, "but will you please untie my hands? I have been very uncomfortable for many hours now."

"Certainly," the inquisitor said. He bent down and released the Cardinal from his bonds. "I want you to be fully relaxed during our conversation this evening."

"Thank you."

"Do you know why we abducted you?"

"I only know what I read in your messages before I was abducted. You consider me to be a spokesman for what you call "the oppressive and intolerant Catholic Church" and you want to silence me as some kind of sign to the world at large."

"That is essentially correct, sir. We regard you as a particularly offensive mouthpiece for an organization that is riddled with scandals and hypocrisy and that opposes the forces of freedom and social justice throughout the world. We want the world to recognize you, and your church, for the sexist, racist and homophobic obstructionists that you are."

"What you think of me is not important," the Cardinal said, "but I sincerely regret your misunderstanding of the Catholic Church. There is so much more to her than the simplistic and inaccurate caricature you have just presented. I pray that you will allow the Holy Spirit to enlighten you concerning the wisdom and holiness of the Catholic faith which remains in spite of the weakness and sins of her individual members—myself included."

"It is I who will enlighten you, sir. Make no mistake."

The inquisitor was unprepared for the Cardinal's humility and his genuine desire to help his captor see with the light of faith.

"Perhaps it's best if you keep quiet for a while and listen to what I have to say," the inquisitor said letting go of all pretended charm.

He walked to the back of the room and picked up a piece of parchment that was lying on top of the desk. It appeared to be some form of declaration or manifesto written in large letters with calligraphy and illuminations similar to the manuscripts copied by monks during medieval times. However, it was clear that this was not an old document but one that was brand new.

"I have here a formal confession that you will sign when our session this evening is concluded," said the inquisitor. "It contains an admission of your church's guilt in three main areas. As the chief justice of your church's Supreme Court, you will take responsibility for all the crimes against humanity committed by your popes and cardinals, bishops and priests down through the ages but particularly in modern times. You will confess to a rigid and outdated moral code, and you will apologize for your intolerance and cruelty to the people you have oppressed—especially women, minorities and those whom you consider to be sexual deviants."

"I have no intention of signing any such document," the Cardinal said. "The whole idea is absurd."

"We'll see about that, sir. Our methods are very persuasive, and you are not a brave man. The red hat you wear is not a martyr's crown."

The Cardinal chose to be silent. He knew that it was

pointless to argue with his inquisitor—especially since his objective was to coerce the Cardinal into betraying the faith.

"First, you will confess to crimes against humanity. History chronicles your church's unforgivable sins from the earliest days of Christianity to the present. The hypocrisy shown by church leaders is unassailable. You impose heavy burdens on others—those least able to oppose you—while you yourselves live luxuriously and indulge all your appetites. Do you deny that churchmen such as yourself are hypocrites guilty of grave offenses against humanity?"

"I deny the sweeping generalizations you have just made. It's true that our Church is made up of ordinary men and women with many faults and weaknesses. The men chosen by our Lord to be his apostles were ordinary, sinful human beings who were converted by his grace and who grew in holiness. Yes, there have been sinful (even wicked) clergy down through the ages. But there have been many more whose lives have born witness to the Gospel of Jesus Christ in powerful, life-giving ways. Your accusations are insulting and unfair to all the holy men and women who have served God's holy Church down through the ages until this very day!"

The inquisitor was visibly shaken by the Cardinal's response. He exploded angrily. "Nonsense, sir! It is your crimes that are offensive to humanity. We will teach you to repent, and we will expose your so-called 'weaknesses' to the whole world!"

The Cardinal remained silent.

"After you confess your church's crimes, you will denounce the rigid moral code that has caused so much anguish for women and men—especially the young—for two millennia. As further evidence of your hypocrisy, you will admit that you have enacted laws that are as unfair and unnatural as they are unenforceable. You forbid young lovers to express their natural sexuality while you allow the old men who run the church to freely engage in practices that your moral code claims are offensive. You prevent people who are divorced and remarried from receiving the sacraments. You excommunicate those who disagree with you on social issues, and you insist on prolonging the lives of sick and elderly people long after all quality and dignity have been lost. Enlightened people in every age have seen through your bourgeois morality, and we have chosen to live as we please in a free society. Now it's time to renounce your oppressive morality once and for all."

"The Church's moral teaching is neither rigid nor oppressive," the Cardinal said softly. "It is based on divine natural and revealed laws. It is intended to bring true freedom and joy to those who follow it. None of us lives the Gospel perfectly, but to the extent we do, Christ's love and peace are with us to set us free!"

"More nonsense! You know nothing of love or freedom—and following your church's moral code is the way to repression and sorrow not joy! I abhor your sanctimonious pronouncements, sir, and I promise you will regret them."

The Cardinal said no more.

"The third and last confession you will make tonight concerns your church's abuse of innocent children, women and gay people. This is perhaps your greatest hypocrisy.

Thousands of pages of Catholic social teaching pretend to speak out in defense of human rights and dignity, and you yourselves are the worst offenders! Gay people seek the right to marry, and you say it is "unnatural" and against God's law. Women defend the right to control their own bodies and to obtain equality in society and in your church, and you block them at every turn. And most hideous of all, children expect protection and care from their pastors, and receive instead the most shameful abuse imaginable. I dare you to defend your church's treatment of these 'little ones' or to justify your cold-hearted rejection of the rights of women and gay people. It cannot be done!"

"I cannot possibly justify evil actions committed by anyone, including priests and bishops," the Cardinal said with a heavy heart. "They will answer to our Lord on the Day of Judgment. But I assure you that the Catholic Church loves and respects *everyone* regardless of gender, sexual orientation, race, ethnicity or social status. It's true that we defend human life from the moment of conception to the moment of natural death—and that we admonish homosexual persons to live the same kind of chaste lives that all unmarried men and women are called to live. We do not discriminate against women or homosexuals. And we reject absolutely and without qualification the physical and sexual abuse of children, elderly people and all who are vulnerable."

"Lies and equivocation! You will sign this confession or subject yourself to a long and painful process of persuasion at the hands of The Sword of Justice!"

The Cardinal looked at his inquisitor with deep

sadness. "As I have already said, I have no intention of signing that document or anything else. I have sworn an oath of fidelity to the truth of our Catholic faith, and I will not betray this oath no matter what you do to me."

"You will regret this obstinacy, sir. We are determined to obtain your signature on this document—one way or another. You will remain here—surely not the kind of accommodations you're used to—until I return. Then you'll be given a choice—sign this confession or submit to the most excruciating, painful torture that can be inflicted on a human being. This meeting is concluded, sir."

The inquisitor abruptly left the room, leaving the Cardinal by himself. The light of day was just beginning to shine through the slits near the ceiling of the old building. The Cardinal immediately fell to his knees and prayed, "Father, if it is possible, let this cup pass from me; yet, not as I will, but as you will" (Mt 26:39).

* * *

Father Mike was having dinner at the Osteria following a meeting with the proprietors, his friends the Norcini brothers, when his cell phone rang. Caller ID told him it was a call from the Cardinal's residence in Rome. He hoped it was Father T calling but when he answered the phone he knew instantly there was trouble. The Cardinal's secretary was calling him at two o'clock in the morning Rome time!

"Father, I'm deeply sorry to disturb you, but Father T has not returned. I called the North American College and Msgr. Leone hasn't returned either. I'm afraid something may have happened to them. Father T never stays out this late."

"You did the right thing calling me," Father Mike said. "I'll place a call to the Vatican Security Office now, and if that doesn't work because of the late hour, I'll call Interpol. Try to get some rest, Sister. I'll call you as soon as I have some information."

"Thank you, Father. I will continue to 'storm heaven' with prayers that nothing happens to the Cardinal, Father T or Msgr. Leone.

Father Mike looked up the number and called Vatican security. As before, he got a recording, but this time he wrote down, and then immediately dialed, the number given to callers to be used *in caso di emergenza*. "If this isn't an emergency, I don't know what is," the priest said out loud. Patrons of the Osteria turned and looked at him, and he realized he was attracting too much attention, so he walked out the front door and stood in the parking lot.

"Do you speak English?" Father Mike asked the gendarme who answered the emergency number.

"*Un po'*," he replied. "A little bit."

"I'm a Catholic priest calling from the United States of America. Two Americans who met with your inspector general this afternoon concerning the Cardinal who has been kidnapped are now missing. You need to alert your superiors right away. Their lives may be at stake. *Capisci quello che ti sto dicendo*," Father Mike demanded. "Do you understand what I'm telling you?"

"*Sì, Padre. Capisco. Certamente.*" The gendarme answered. "I really do understand, Father"

"Good. Then please call your superiors immediately. I'll call back later to find out if there are any developments. *Ciao*."

Next, Father Mike called Msgr. Leone's sister Clare. He didn't want to alarm her, but he thought it was important to find out if she had heard anything from her brother.

"No, Father. He hasn't called. That's really unlike him, and I'm beginning to worry."

"I'm sure Msgr. Leone and Father T are OK, Clare, but we're not taking any chances," Father Mike said in his most reassuring pastoral voice. "I've placed a call to Vatican security. They'll let us know as soon as they track them down."

"Thank you, Father. I'm not going to say anything to anyone about this. No sense worrying people unnecessarily."

"A wise decision, Clare. I'll let you know as soon I hear something."

Father Mike made two more calls while standing in the Osteria's parking lot. First, he called Father T's niece, Anna. Then he called his friend's cousin, Msgr. Vincent Cugino. He left voice messages for both telling them it was about Father T and asking them to call as soon as they received this message.

When Father Mike returned to the restaurant, the Norcini brothers brought him his dinner, which they had kept warm for him. He had no appetite for anything now, but he made a largely unsuccessful effort to eat in consideration of his friends' kindness.

"Something about this whole business doesn't sit right," the priest said to his friends. "Sal's been in tight spots before, but never this far away from home. And never with international terrorists in the picture!"

Father Mike's next call was to Marisa, Father's travel

consultant.

"When's the very next flight to Rome?" he asked in a tone of voice that Marisa recognized immediately as deadly serious.

"Is Father T OK?"

"I honestly don't know, Marisa. I may have to go to Rome to find out, and I'd like to know what my options are."

"Well, Father, the earliest I can get you there is the day after tomorrow. You can take a Delta flight at 10:45 tomorrow morning through Atlanta that arrives in Rome at 7:30 in the morning. But it will cost $2,500 for coach, and, of course, the ticket won't be refundable."

"Are there plenty of seats available? If so, then let's wait until first thing tomorrow morning. If not, go ahead and book it."

"We can wait until tomorrow morning, Father, until about 8:30. That will still give you just over two hours. Jessie Lindbergh, Father T's parishioner who manages the airport, can help you get through security without any delays."

"Thank you, Marisa. What would we do without you?"

"Just get Father T home safely, Father Mike. That's all I ask!"

* * *

Father T and Msgr. Leone arrived in Naples around midnight local time—about an hour after the inquisitor's private jet landed. They had been blindfolded and had their hands and feet bound with plastic strips during the entire two-hour trip from Rome. For some reason, the two "thugs" who transported them failed to take their cell phones. Father T's phone vibrated in his shirt pocket several times during the trip as Father Mike and his niece Anna tried desperately to reach him. Msgr. Leone's cell phone vibrated once in his pants pocket, and he assumed it was his sister Clare wondering why she hadn't heard from him.

Traffic in the city was minimal due to the late hour, but the back streets of Napoli were still full of people. The driver maneuvered the narrow streets carefully and arrived without difficulty at the ancient building that served as the Cardinal's prison and place of interrogation. Before they let Msgr. Leone and Father T out of the SUV, the driver went inside to seek instructions while the other "thug" stayed behind and kept watch.

"You can take these blindfolds off now," Father T said. "We know where we are. This is obviously some back alley in Naples."

His abductor did not respond.

"Mi, *capisci?* Father T asked. "Do you understand me?"

Still no response.

When the driver returned, he opened the back door and removed the blindfolds but not the thin strips of plastic that bound their wrists.

"*Scendete!*" said the thug. "Get out now!"

"Where are you taking us?" Msgr. Leone asked gently but firmly.

"To join your friend the cardinal and witness his humiliation. Now get out of the vehicle and go through that door."

The door led into a long, dark hallway with a strong

odor that they later learned was the result of the building's many years of service as an armory. The oil used to clean and lubricate firearms had seeped into the walls and floors over the years giving the building a distinctive (and, apparently, permanent) smell.

When they arrived at the storage room where the Cardinal was being held, the two thugs opened the door and then removed the strips that bound the hands of the two Americans. The room was empty except for the mattress of straw and the chamber pot.

"Where's the Cardinal?" Father T asked. In fact, he was still locked in the office where the grand inquisitor had interrogated him.

"*Sta in arrivo*," said one of the thugs. "He'll be here soon enough."

The two men left and locked the door behind them.

"What do we do now?" Msgr. Leone asked. "This place is really creepy."

"I'm going to call the chief inspector if I can get a signal. I think it's time to use the code and ask the Holy Family to help us all get out of here!"

Unfortunately, there was no cell reception in the old armory building with its thick stone walls and its high ceilings. *Nessun servizio* was the only message Father T's Italian phone would give him in spite of his repeated, unsuccessful efforts to call out.

"Jesus, Mary and Joseph!" the priest exclaimed, his words bouncing off the ancient stones, echoing like a chorus of monks chanting their evening prayers.

"Let's hope the Cardinal joins us soon," Msgr. Leone said. "I sure hope he's OK."

"The Sacred Heart will help us get out of here," Father said—as much to himself as to his old friend. "He's never let me down yet!"

The two Americans sat down on the straw and waited for their former archbishop. They tried as best they could to prepare themselves for a long hard night.

IL SETTIMO GIORNO

IL SETTIMO GIORNO.
MATTINATA.
(Day Seven. Morning)

Interpol's chief inspector had arrived in Naples just before the plane carrying The Sword of Justice's grand inquisitor, and he waited with two local agents before following him from the Naples airport to the place where the Cardinal was being held captive. Once they arrived at the old armory building, the Interpol agents attempted to setup a station where they could conduct surveillance. Unfortunately, the building's thick stone walls had the same effect on their sophisticated equipment as they did on Father T's cell phone. *Nessun servizio!* Nothing worked, including the bugs planted on Father T and Msgr. Leone prior to their visit to Harry's Bar.

The chief inspector was not pleased.

"We only have two choices," he said to the two agents who were with him. "We either break in there and risk the lives of three innocent people, or we stay out here and wait—without any idea what's going on in there! Surround the building and set up SWAT teams on the roofs. We have to be prepared for the worst."

Father T and Msgr. Leone slept fitfully on the straw. They had had no contact with anyone through the night, and although they tried to stay awake, eventually they both had to give in and get some rest.

The Cardinal, left alone in the interrogation room, prayed through the night, desperately asking the Lord for courage and wisdom. He was not sure what the grand inquisitor had in store for him, but he knew it would be more painful than anything he had ever experienced.

"My enemy is right," the Cardinal said to himself, and to his Lord. "I am not a brave man. But with the help of God's grace, I will do my very best to stay true to my faith and my vocation."

The inquisitor spent the night in another part of the building in a makeshift bedroom that was a lot more comfortable than the rooms occupied by his American guests. Still, the mattress was hard and the room was damp and cold. When he woke up, he was in an especially foul mood.

"It's time to obtain the cardinal's confession and get out of here—for good!" the terrorist leader said to his henchmen.

"I'm afraid we have a serious problem," one of the men said. "The building is surrounded by Interpol agents. They must have followed us here from Rome."

"Fools!" the inquisitor exclaimed. "How could you be so stupid? I told you to take every precaution. Now we'll have to use the Americans as hostages and bargain our way out of here. One way or another, I'm going to use that cardinal to embarrass the Roman church!"

At the inquisitor's command, the Cardinal was removed from the room where he spent the night. He assumed he was being taken somewhere to be tortured, so he was very surprised when his captors returned him to the room with the straw mattress. He was even more surprised—astonished, in fact—when he discovered

Father T and Msgr. Leone lying in the straw fast asleep.

The two men opened the door just wide enough for the Cardinal to enter and quickly closed it behind him. They had not replaced the plastic strips the inquisitor removed, so he had full use of all his limbs.

The Cardinal knelt down next to Father T and gently nudged him.

"Sal, what on earth are you doing here? And why is Bill Leone with you?"

Msgr. Leone opened his eyes before Father T. He was thrilled to see the Cardinal who was obviously alive and unharmed.

"Your Eminence, God bless you. We were scared to death. Thank God you're not hurt—are you?"

"I'm fine, Bill. For now. What are you and Msgr. Turiddu doing here?"

"I can answer that," Father T said as he rubbed his eyes and stretched. "We promised the archbishop, and all your friends back home, that no harm would come to you. End of story."

"You mean you came all the way over here just to find me? That was very foolish—and extremely dangerous. The men who abducted me hate the Catholic Church. We are all in great jeopardy."

"The Sacred Heart is with us, Your Eminence," Father T said. "I have no doubt he will help us find a way out of here."

"Well, we better start looking for a way out now," Msgr. Leone said. "There's no telling how much time we have before those goons come back."

The three Americans searched the room carefully,

pressing against walls and looking for trap doors in the flooring. Nothing. The only way out was through the very thick, very locked door.

"What about the slits in the ceiling?" Father T asked. "Is there any way one of us could get up there to see if any of the slits are loose?"

"Doubtful," the Cardinal said. "We could probably move those pallets that are lined against the far wall and stack them on top of each other, but there's no telling how old they are or whether they would support our weight."

"I'm the lightest, most agile person here," Father T said. "I'm willing to give it a try."

"With all due respect, Sal, you're not the oldest person here," Msgr. Leone pointed out. "I'm your senior, even if it's only by two months, and there's no way I'm going to let you climb up to the ceiling on old wooden pallets. I'll not take any guff from you. I'm going up."

"Let's not waste any time then," Father T said with a scowl. "Let's stack the pallets and get started."

With the Cardinal's help, Msgr. Leone and Father T began stacking the pallets so that they formed stairs leading up to the ceiling. Msgr. Leone led the way, and as he placed the pallets on top of each other, he gradually (and gingerly) ascended with them. The wood pallets bent and creaked under his weight, but they didn't break. Before long, he was high enough, and close enough, to reach out and grab hold of the slits in the ceiling.

As Msgr. Leone reached out to try and test the slits, the pallets began to wobble.

"Steady!" the Cardinal called out. "Don't make any sudden moves!"

The priest froze, and the wobbling pallets settled down. He waited for what seemed like forever before trying to grab the slits again.

"I don't think there's any give here," Msgr. Leone said to the Cardinal and Father T. "I would really have to work at shaking these loose, and there's no way these pallets would stand still for that."

Just then, Msgr. Leone felt his cell phone vibrate in his pants pocket. The unexpected movement startled him, and he froze again. The vibrations continued.

"My cell phone works!" the priest shouted. "It must be because I'm closer to the outside."

"Answer it!" Father T called up to him. "Tell whoever's calling to alert the *polizia*."

Msgr. Leone was able to get to his phone just in time. It was the chief inspector of Interpol.

"Are you OK? How about Father T and the Cardinal?"

"We're all fine, Inspector, but we're locked in a storage room in a big old building in Naples."

"I know exactly where you are, *Monsignore*. We have the building surrounded with snipers on the roof tops, but we didn't want to take any action until we knew you were unharmed. Can you tell me what room you're in—in which section of the building?"

"I can't describe it for you, Inspector. It was too dark when we arrived here, and my sense of direction is all turned around."

"Any clue would really help us locate you, *Monsignore*. If we know where you are, we have a much better chance of ensuring your safety."

"Well, I happen to be close to the window slats near

the ceiling. This is the only place we can get cell phone reception, but I can't stay here long. The pallets I'm standing on are not too sturdy."

"Can you drop something from the window—to show us where you are?"

"All I have is this cell phone and my wallet. Wait. I think I have some prayer cards in my wallet. I'll see if I can shove them out the window."

While balancing precariously on the old wooden pallets, Msgr. Leone reached into his pocket and removed his wallet. Sure enough, there were four prayer cards, which he removed with one hand while using the other hand to hold the cell phone. The Cardinal and Father T watched carefully. They were silently preparing to try catch their friend if any of the pallets he was standing on suddenly collapsed.

"I have them," he said to the Inspector. "I'm pushing them through the slits now."

Four prayer cards floated to the ground below, and one of the Interpol agents ran down the alley to retrieve them.

"We see them!" the inspector said. "Now that we know your exact location, we can proceed with our plans. I'll call you as soon as we're ready."

"Inspector, I can't stay up here on these pallets, and I won't receive your call after I climb back down to the main floor. Can we arrange some other kind of signal?"

"We'll reverse the process. Once we're ready to move, one of the snipers on the roof will push something through the slits. When you see something drop down, you'll know we're on our way. Stay as far away from the doors as you can in case there's an exchange of gunfire."

"*Grazie*, Inspector. We'll wait for your signal."

Msgr. Leone moved quickly (but gently) down to the floor. Father T and the Cardinal held the pallets until they were sure their friend was safe.

"Interpol is planning to 'storm the Bastille,' " Msgr. Leone said. "As soon as we see something drop from the ceiling, we're supposed to move as far away from the door as possible in case of gunfire."

"Jesus, Mary and Joseph!" Father T exclaimed. "I hope they know what they're doing."

"I'm sorry I got you into this," the Cardinal said. "I still can't believe you came all the way over here to rescue me. I will always be grateful."

"There's nothing to do now but wait," Msgr. Leone said.

"And pray," the Cardinal added.

"Well, I'm much better at praying than waiting," Father T mumbled to himself. "Sacred Heart of Jesus, please don't let us down now."

IL SETTIMO GIORNO.
MEZZOGIORNO.
(Day Seven. Noon)

It was noontime in Italy but 5 a.m. back home. Father Mike was up early, packing for what he hoped would be a very quick trip to Rome.

He was startled when his cell phone rang so early in the morning. Caller ID displayed an unfamiliar number, but Father Mike recognized it as a Vatican exchange.

"Pronto e buon giorno," Father Mike answered.

"Giorno, Padre. This is the chief inspector of Vatican security. I understand that you called us concerning Father T and Msgr. Leone."

"Yes, *Signore.* We have not heard from either of them for some time now. We're very concerned about their safety. Of course, we're also very worried about the Cardinal."

"I'm sorry to inform you that at present all three of your friends are being held by members of a terrorist group, The Sword of Justice, in a former armory building in *Napoli.* Although we have not yet had contact with their leaders, we consider this a potential hostage situation. Interpol and the local *polizia* are on the scene. We're prepared to negotiate, but we're also ready to use force if necessary."

"I certainly hope that the safety of the hostages is your first priority, Inspector."

"Certo, caro Padre," the inspector said. "Their safety

comes first!"

"I am packing my suitcase now, Inspector. I will arrive in Rome at 8:30 tomorrow morning—your time. I'll see if I can arrange a transfer to Naples."

"*Padre*, with all due respect, there is nothing you can do here. We are doing everything possible. Please remain where you are. I promise to keep you informed of our progress."

"I'm afraid you don't understand, Inspector. There is absolutely no way that I can remain here as long as my friends are in danger. Father T taught me better than that. I'm coming, Inspector, no matter what."

"*Si, Capisco.* It is the Sicilian way."

"I'm not Sicilian," Father Mike said. "But many of my friends are, and I've learned over the years that in some cases, the Sicilian way is the best way!"

"Have a safe trip, *Padre. Ciao.*"

* * *

The wait was interminable. Nothing was happening, and that made Father T nervous. He paced the length of the store room and then began moving the pallets to form a kind of barrier, like the forts his brothers' children used to make out of empty boxes in the basement of his family's pecan factory. These pallets were very much like the ones his family used (with forklifts) to transport boxes filled with pecans to the delivery trucks that shipped them all over the country.

"I wish I knew what was going on," the priest said to no one in particular. "I'm tempted to climb up to the ceiling and call the inspector. I sure wish I knew what they're planning."

"Patience, Father. As you said earlier, the Sacred Heart is in charge now—not us."

"Yes, your Eminence, you're right, of course. It's just that I was raised to believe that the Lord helps those who help themselves. Surrender has never been part of my vocabulary!"

"I know, Sal. I know. But in the spiritual life abandonment to Divine Providence—some call it joyful surrender—is not something quitters do. It requires courage, a steadfast faith, and the confidence to let God decide what is best for us. That's hard for all of us, I know, but sometimes it's our only choice."

"Jesus, Mary and Joseph!" Father T exclaimed. "I sure wish the Inspector would hurry up and do whatever he's going to do."

"I think maybe you're right, Sal," Msgr. Leone said as he began climbing back up the makeshift staircase. "I'm going to call the inspector."

When he got as high as he could go, he dialed the inspector's number. Unfortunately, it went right to voicemail. He decided to wait a few minutes and try again. Father T and the Cardinal stood at the base steadying the pallets and preparing to catch their friend (or at least break his fall) if anything went wrong.

After a few minutes, Msgr. Leone's cell phone vibrated. It was the chief inspector.

"*Monsignore*, I am so happy you picked up. I was speaking to your captor, the so-called grand inquisitor, when you called. He insists that the Cardinal sign his confession or all of you will die. We can storm the building, but it is built like a fortress, as you know, and we could not guarantee your safety."

"I'll let the Cardinal know," Msgr. Leone said. "But there's no way he'll sign any document that falsely implicates himself or denigrates the Church."

"I know that the Cardinal is a man of principle, but there are times when we must do the lesser of two evils. I believe this is one of those times, *Monsignore*."

"I'm not about to lecture His Eminence on ethics," Msgr. Leone said. "But I'll give him your message. *Ciao*, Inspector."

"*In boca al lupo*," said the Inspector. "I wish you well, *Monsignore*—especially in this very difficult situation."

As the 82-year-old monsignor slowly descended, the pallets began to rattle and shake in spite of his friends' best efforts to steady them. Before he was on solid footing, they all came tumbling down like the walls of Jericho responding to Joshua's trumpets. Fortunately, Msgr. Leone was not hurt, but the guards must have been standing right outside the door, because they immediately unlocked it and came rushing into the room. What they saw was Msgr. Leone sprawled out on the floor surrounded by pallets with the Cardinal and Father T reaching down to him to help him up.

The grand inquisitor followed his henchmen into the room.

"Attempting to escape? I assure you that even if you had climbed all the way up to the top you would have discovered that there is no way out. You are our prisoners until I decide either to let you go or to bestow your martyrs' crowns. The choice is entirely yours," the inquisitor said holding up the parchment he had shown the Cardinal the night before. "Either you persuade your friend the Cardinal to sign this document, or all of you will die."

"*Giammai!*" Father T shouted. "The Cardinal will never sign your ridiculous confession."

"Father T is correct," the Cardinal said. "Under no circumstances—including torture and death—will I sign anything you give me. I regret that my friends are here with me, and I beg you most earnestly to let them go and keep only me, but nothing you do to any of us will compel me to sign that blasphemous document."

"You will all regret this stubbornness. I assure you The Sword of Justice will strike—one way or another!"

The inquisitor and his companions left the room, locking the door behind them. The Cardinal sat down on the straw mattress and tried to collect his thoughts. Father T and Msgr. Leone quietly began to pick up the pallets that had been upended and scattered throughout the room. When they finished, they each sat down on a pallet and waited.

IL SETTIMO GIORNO.
SERA.
(Day Seven. Afternoon)

Father Mike got a ride to the airport from his good friends Bart and Mike Norcini.

"Just drop me off," Father Mike said. "There's no reason to pay for short-term parking."

"Not a chance," said Bart who was driving. "We're going to make sure you have a proper sendoff."

When they entered the terminal, Father Mike went straight to the ticket counter to check-in for the international flight. He didn't check any luggage. He deliberately packed light, with only a carry-on bag and a briefcase, but the ticket agent needed to see his passport before he could be issued a boarding pass for his connecting flight to Rome.

When he turned to say goodbye to the Norcini brothers before going through security, he noticed that Bart and Mike were talking with two priests and two women. The priests were Father T's cousin, Msgr. Vincent Cugino, and his good friend, Msgr. John Dutzow. Father Mike recognized the women as Msgr. Leone's sister Clare, Father T's niece Anna Dominica, and his parishioner the airport manager, Jesse Lindbergh.

"What are you all doing here?" Father Mike asked.

"John and I are going with you," Msgr. Cugino answered. "Anna and Jesse helped make the arrangements."

"What? How can you guys go with me? Who'll cover Masses, funerals and sick calls at your parishes?"

"I talked to the Abbot," Anna said. "I explained the situation and he said the monks at the Abbey would cover the two parishes for as long as it takes. They love Father T as much as we do, and they would do anything to help him out now that he's in trouble. Now it's up to you guys to bring my uncle and Msgr. Leone home in one piece. If you don't, you'll have me to deal with!"

"Me, too," Clare said. "But seriously, Fathers, I really appreciate what you're doing. Please bring Father T and my brother Bill home to us as soon as possible!"

After they all said goodbye to Clare and Anna (thanking her for making it possible for the two pastors to leave their parishes for an uncertain period of time), Jesse escorted the three priests through airport security.

"There's no way you can avoid going through security," she said. "But I'll make sure you get through the line quickly with no hassles."

"Thank you, Jesse. How did you know we were coming?" Msgr. Dutzow asked.

"Marisa, called me right after you asked her to make the travel arrangements for you and Father Vince. By the way, she asked me to tell you that all three of you are booked on a flight to Naples 90 minutes after you arrive in Rome. I've called ahead to the management at Rome's Leonardo da Vinci Airport. They'll make sure you make your connection."

"Thank you, Jesse," Msgr. Cugino said. "Father T will be very grateful—and so are we."

The flight to Atlanta was on time and uneventful. The three priests had plenty of time to walk 14 gates, take the escalator down, ride the shuttle train from Concourse D to Concourse E, take the escalator up and, finally, walk seven more gates to their destination.

"I can see why Sal refuses to go through Atlanta," Msgr. Dutzow said. "It's a real workout changing planes here!"

"We're lucky we were able to get any seats at all on such short notice," Father Mike said. "Beggars can't be choosers. Thank God for Marisa. She not only got us on the plane, she managed to assign us to seats in the Economy Comfort section so we have a little extra legroom."

When they were settled into their seats on the flight to Rome, Msgr. Cugino suggested that they spend a few minutes in silent prayer for the Cardinal, Father T and Msgr. Leone. "Lord, make this trip a waste of time," he prayed. "Show us when we get there that we weren't needed after all. We'll eat some pasta, drink some wine, and then come home again!"

Shortly after boarding was complete, the Airbus A 330-300 taxied down the runway and took off with nearly 300 passengers who were eager to visit (or return home to) the Italian peninsula. Three of those passengers were Catholic priests on a special mission—to make sure that the Cardinal was safe and that Father T and his old friend Bill Leone returned home safely.

"This reminds me of a funny story I heard at one of the national Knights of Columbus conventions," Msgr. Dutzow said to his two companions once they had reached cruising altitude and the flight attendant had served them drinks.

"Two bishops took a twin engine puddle jumper across Lake Michigan on their way from South Bend, Indiana (Notre Dame) to Chicago (their home town). Halfway across the lake, one of the engines caught fire and had to be shut down. The pilot made an announcement assuring his passengers that they were perfectly capable of making it to Chicago's lakefront airport with one engine. 'Besides,' the pilot said, 'we have two bishops on board with us.' A sweet little old lady seated in the back row was then heard to say, 'I'd rather have two engines!' "

"Finish your drink, John," Msgr. Cugino said. "It's going to be a long flight."

* * *

Father T was fit to be tied. His patience was exhausted. He had been pacing the room for what seemed like hours. The Cardinal and Msgr. Leone tried to reassure him, but his Sicilian blood was boiling, and he knew he had to act!

"This is insanity. I'm going to get us out of here."

Before his two companions could stop him, Father T was banging on the door.

"I want to see the head honcho. Open this door. Now!"

The Cardinal and Msgr. Leone could hardly believe it when the door opened and Father T was escorted out of the storage room.

"Stop! Where are you taking him?" Msgr. Leone demanded, but it was too late. Before they knew what was happening, Father T was on his way to see the grand inquisitor.

"I hope he knows what he's up against," Msgr. Leone said. "He's a tough character."

"Which one?" the Cardinal asked. "The inquisitor or Father T?"

* * *

Interpol had set up a command center in a small store across from the armory's front door. Agents, supported by *Carabinieri*, blocked the alley behind the building, and snipers were placed on the rooftops covering all sides of the old fortress. No one was getting in or out without the authorities knowing it.

The chief inspector was worried because there still was no substantive communication from The Sword of Justice members inside. Except for his brief conversation with the grand inquisitor, followed by his phone call with Msgr. Leone, which assured him that the three Americans had not been harmed, he had no information and no effective plan for the safe return of the hostages.

A crowd began to form around the perimeter. Neighbors and local citizens were expected, but this crowd was different. There were bearded monks from Norcia wearing black habits who were determined to help rescue the Cardinal who had been snatched from their monastery while they slept. And Vatican officials were on-site, too, because they were deeply concerned about one of their highest ranking prelates and his two friends from the United States. Finally, there were four young men who were not known to any of the local police, but who looked like they meant business. A Naples policeman who overheard them talking said that he thought their dialect was Sicilian, but he couldn't say for sure.

"This is going to be a long day," the chief inspector said to the field officer who was stationed with him across the street from the armory's front door. "The crowd outside keeps getting bigger, and so far we have nothing to show for our efforts."

IL SETTIMO GIORNO.
NOTTE.
(Day Seven. Late Night)

It was late by the time Father T came back to the storage room. He had been gone for more than four hours, and the Cardinal and Msgr. Leone were worried sick.

"What happened?" Msgr. Leone asked. "What have you been doing all this time?"

"Did you meet with the inquisitor?" the Cardinal added. "I hope he was more respectful to you than he was to me."

Father T smiled. "It's all taken care of. We'll be out of here by morning."

"Are you sure?" Msgr. Leone asked.

"What did you say to him?" the Cardinal inquired. "Are you sure you trust him?"

"Of course I don't trust him, but I helped him understand what would happen to him and to his goons if any harm came to Your Eminence or to Bill or me. He doesn't fear Interpol or the Naples *polizia*, but I helped him understand how my family in Sicily would handle a situation like this. I told a few stories that I picked up on my trips to visit my cousins. They were very persuasive."

"I don't believe it," Msgr. Leone said. "Are you serious?"

"While I was talking to the grand pooh-bah, one of his thugs came in and told him about the crowds that have gathered outside this building. Apparently we're not only surrounded by *Carabinieri*, there are also hundreds of other people lining the streets and alleyways—including some native sons of Sicily, most likely my cousins!"

"But how would your cousins—or anyone else—know we're here?" the Cardinal asked.

"My family is very well-connected. Any communication from Interpol or the Vatican or the Naples *polizia* concerning me would find its way to a member of my family sooner or later. Besides, before Bill and I left for the meeting at Harry's Bar, I made a few phone calls. I told Michael O' Keefe at the NAC that if I didn't call him last night he should have his rector call Vatican security. I also asked him to call my cousins and let them know I was in trouble. "

"That's amazing, Sal. I knew you were well-connected back home, but I never guessed you'd have the same kind of network here in Italy."

"We Turiddus stick together. It's the Sicilian way. Threaten one member of our family—anywhere in the world—and you've insulted us all."

The Cardinal said he was tired—and very hungry. None of them had been fed all day, and there was only one small jug of water. "I hope you're right, Sal. I'd really like all of us to get out of here soon!"

L'OTTAVO GIORNO

L'OTTAVO GIORNO.
MATTINATA.
(The Eighth Day. Morning)

The Delta Airlines flight carrying Father T's cousin Vince and his friends John and Mike arrived on time. As Jesse promised, two representatives of the Rome airport authority met them as they disembarked and guided them smoothly through passport control and customs. The three priests only had carry-on luggage so there was no waiting at baggage claim.

The plane to Naples was scheduled to depart from the Domestic Terminal, so the airport officials escorted them on a private shuttle bus from the International Terminal to a special entrance just beyond their gate. Marisa had made sure they all had boarding documents, so the transition was as quick and uneventful as possible.

As they waited at the gate for the Alitalia flight to *Napoli*, Father Mike called the inspector general of Vatican security to let him know they arrived safely and to inquire about the status of the Cardinal, Father T. and Msgr. Leone.

"*Sì, Padre,*" the head of security said. "I'm happy you arrived safely. Two gendarmes from my staff will meet you at the Naples airport and bring you to the site where His Eminence and your friends are being held hostage."

"Are they OK?" Father Mike asked.

"*Certo.* All of the reports we have received indicate that no one has been harmed. We expect to hear something significant from the terrorists' leader soon. We hope that we will be able to negotiate with him. If not, Interpol and the Naples polizia will know what to do."

"I certainly hope you're right, Inspector. My friends and I have come a very long way. We desperately want a peaceful solution to this crisis."

"As do we, Father. As do we."

* * *

Father T and Msgr. Leone had insisted that the Cardinal sleep on the straw mattress, while they both slept on the floor. The Cardinal wouldn't hear of it. He proposed that they each take turns—three hours apiece. In the morning, their captors brought hard rolls and coffee, which the Cardinal blessed and the three Americans consumed rapidly and in silence.

"I wish we could celebrate Mass," Father T said. "I can't remember a time when I went two days in a row without receiving the holy Eucharist. We need the grace of the sacrament of Christ's body and blood more than ever right now."

"I agree," said Msgr. Leone. "I can't wait to get out of here so we can all go back to our daily routines!"

The door opened and two men came in followed by their leader.

"Monsignor Turiddu, we have confirmed what you told us about your family. We do not want any problems. In a few minutes, I will speak to the chief inspector of Interpol who has taken up residence across the street. I will make him a very simple proposal: In exchange for safe passage to the port of Naples, and a one-way ticket to Stockholm, we will release you and your American friend unharmed. The Cardinal, on the other hand, will accompany us to The Sword of Justice headquarters in Sweden. There he will be persuaded to either sign the confession we have prepared for him or suffer the consequences."

"No deal," Father T said. "Msgr. Leone and I are not going anywhere without the Cardinal. And nothing you can say or do will change our minds. End of story!"

"That's right," Msgr. Leone said. "We came here to free the Cardinal, and we're not leaving unless he goes with us."

"You Americans are such fools. What about you, Reverend Cardinal, are you going to let your friends share your martyr's crown?"

"I wish you would let them go, and I wish I could persuade them to leave me with you. But I must insist, once again, that nothing you say or do will compel me to sign that document. My position on this matter is absolutely non-negotiable."

The grand inquisitor turned bright red and tossed the document he was holding at the Cardinal's face.

"You will sign this confession or you will die. The choice is yours."

* * *

Two Vatican gendarmes met Msgr. Cugino, Msgr. Dutzow and Father Belcamp at their arrival gate in *Napoli*. The three priests were tired and hungry, but they declined the gendarmes offer to stop at an airport café and insisted they be taken to the armory immediately. The streets of

Naples were crowded, but the gendarme who drove their vehicle was obviously skilled at maneuvering big city streets in Italy.

"This is my first time in Naples," Msgr. Dutzow said. "It's really dirty."

"And dangerous," Msgr. Cugino added.

When they reached a roadblock several streets from the armory, the driver told them they would have to walk the rest of the way. The driver stayed with the vehicle, but the second gendarme accompanied them on foot.

"This street is called *Spaccanapoli*," the gendarme said. "Actually, it has several street names that change constantly, but because it divides the *centro storico*, the city center, in half it is generally called 'splitting Naples' (*spaccanapoli*)."

"How far are we from the armory?" Father Mike asked.

"We must first pass the cathedral, *il Duomo*, with its world-famous Chapel of St. Gennaro," the gendarme said. "Then it is only two blocks south. We will be there very soon."

"Good," Msgr. Cugino said. "I can't wait to get my hands on those terrorists. We Sicilians know how to handle our enemies."

When the three priests and their Vatican escort arrived at the scene, they were amazed. The crowd had swelled to what seemed like hundreds of people. There was no room for all those people, so they backed into doorways and leaned out of second and third story windows.

"Who are all these people?" Msgr. Dutzow asked the gendarme.

"I honestly don't know, *Padre*. Some of them are curious by-standers, but others—like those young men with the angry looks—clearly mean business!"

The priests were taken to the chief inspector of Interpol. He had been informed by Vatican security that they were coming, but he frankly considered their presence a distraction he didn't need.

"You are welcome, Fathers, but please stay out of the way. We have a very tense situation here. Your friends' lives will depend on how well we are able to negotiate with these terrorists.

* * *

The grand inquisitor paced back and forth in his makeshift office. He was determined to obtain the Cardinal's signature or risk embarrassing himself and making his mission a complete failure. Father T was a wildcard he had not anticipated. Members of the Naples chapter of The Sword of Justice were outside mingling with the crowd. They called the inquisitor with regular updates on the number of Interpol agents, *polizia*, and snipers on the rooftops. None of these concerned the inquisitor greatly. What really bothered him was the group of young men— either Sicilians or *Napoletani* or both—who lined the streets and were growing in number. Father T had warned him that his extended family would know what to do if anything happened to the three Americans. The inquisitor feared (in his bones) that the Sicilian priest was not exaggerating.

Out of desperation, the inquisitor picked up the telephone and called Interpol. In his previous conversation with the chief inspector, he resisted Interpol's efforts to engage him in substantive conversation. Now he was prepared to state his terms.

"To whom am I speaking?" the inquisitor asked once the receptionist had transferred him to the Command Center across from the armory. The chief inspector identified himself.

"Yes, Inspector, as you know, I am the Grand Inquisitor of The Sword of Justice. I am in charge here, and I want to present you with my terms. They are not negotiable."

"Please proceed, sir, but keep in mind that we have your building completely surrounded. We do not want anyone harmed," the chief inspector said, "but we cannot allow this stalemate to continue."

"My terms are simple. We will release the two American priests in exchange for safe passage for me, my two associates and the cardinal. We wish to be taken to the *Molo Beverello*, the port of Naples, where a ship will be waiting to take us to our homeland. Once we arrive safely, the cardinal will be released—assuming, of course, that he confesses to his church's many crimes against humanity."

"It will take us some time to make these arrangements," the chief inspector said. "In the meantime, we will require proof that the Cardinal and his friends have not been harmed. Will you allow me to come inside—unarmed of course—to speak with the Americans and verify that they are OK?"

"Not you, Inspector, or any member of the law enforcement community. Select a volunteer from the vast crowd outside. Any innocent bystander who's brave enough to join us is welcome. I promise that if he behaves no harm will come to him."

"I cannot allow another innocent person to become

involved in this, sir. We already have too many potential casualties."

"Then you must be content with my assurance that the three Americans are unharmed. Good day, Inspector."

Father T was getting restless again. He was sure that his conversation with the grand inquisitor had convinced the terrorists of the foolishness of keeping the three of them locked up in this place, and he couldn't understand what was causing the delay. The Cardinal and Msgr. Leone urged patience, but Father T was not buying it.

"I can't understand why the Sacred Heart is allowing this insanity to continue. We need to get out of here—now!"

"I remember reading an article by a spiritual writer concerning the Sacred Heart. He said that the heart of Jesus is so large and all encompassing that we can never fully comprehend it. I'm quite sure that our Lord has a plan for us," the Cardinal continued. "We just don't understand it yet."

"I'm going to climb back up to the ceiling," Msgr. Leone said. "Maybe the chief inspector can tell us what's happening. Will you steady the pallets for me?"

"Just be careful," the Cardinal said. "We thought we were going to lose you the last time."

Once again, Msgr. Leone gently ascended the make-shift stairway. When he got near the top, he called the chief inspector.

"*Pronto, Monsignore*, is everything well?"

"As well as can be expected, Inspector. Can you give us

any information about how long we have to remain here?"

"We are negotiating with your friend the grand inquisitor, but he still insists that the Cardinal must go with them to Sweden and that he sign that ridiculous confession. Without that, he refuses to release you and Father T."

"I don't understand, Inspector. Father T and the Cardinal have both told him—in no uncertain terms—that what he wants will never happen. Are you prepared to deal with this situation by force if necessary? I'm afraid I can't see any other way."

"We are prepared for many different possibilities, *Monsignore*. But, of course, your safety is our first priority."

"Thank you, Inspector. Please let us know if there's anything we can do from the inside."

"*Certo, Monsignore, certo*. By the way, you should know that three of your priest friends from America are here in Naples."

"What? Who?"

"Msgr. Cugino, Msgr. Dutzow and Father Belcamp," the inspector said. "Un attimo, Monsignore, I will put Msgr. Cugino on the line."

"Bill, are you OK? How are Father T and the Cardinal? What kind of mess have you guys gotten yourselves into?"

"We're fine, Vince, but what are you all doing here? I can't believe it. Hang on a second while I tell Father T and the Cardinal."

Msgr. Leone called down to Father T and the Cardinal to tell them that their good friends from back home were here in Naples.

"Huh?" Father T said. "Do you mean that Vince and John and Mike are actually here in Naples now?"

"Yes, Father. They're right across the street waiting for us to get out safely."

"Jesus, Mary and Joseph! I never would have believed it."

"I hope they stay where they are," the Cardinal said. "I'm responsible for too many of you as it is!"

"I have an idea," Father T said. "I want to talk to Vince."

"We won't get any cell reception down there, Father, and I don't think you should come up here."

"Nonsense!" Father T nearly shouted. "I'm as agile as a mountain goat. Tell Vince I'll call him back in a few minutes. Then come down here so I can take your place."

"OK, Sal."

Msgr. Cugino handed the phone back to the chief inspector.

"Msgr. Leone says that Father T will call back in a few minutes. He wants to talk to me."

It wasn't long before the inspector's cell phone rang, and Father T's cousin answered it.

"Yes, Sal, it's me. Are you OK? What about the Cardinal? How's he taking all this?"

"We're fine, Vinnie, but there's no time for chitchat. Go out to the street and find our cousins from Sicily. Tell them it's time to end all this insanity and get us out of here."

"Our cousins? What are they doing here?"

"I told Mike O'Keefe, one of our seminarians at the NAC, to call Gioacchino if he didn't hear from me yesterday. I figured Gioacchino would get in touch with our cousins in Sicily. The grand pooh-bah here told me that four of them were out on the street."

"OK, Sal, but what are they going to do?"

"I have absolutely no idea, but I have complete confidence in our family's ability to settle this thing once and for all."

"No violence, Sal. Please."

"I hope not, Vinnie, but it's time to get us out of here. One way or another. End of story!"

"OK, Sal. Please be careful."

"I will, Vince. Thank you."

Msgr. Cugino handed the cell phone back to the chief inspector and said he was going out for some air. Father Mike and Msgr. Dutzow offered to go with him, but he declined saying, "This is family business. I have to do this alone."

About five minutes later, Msgr. Cugino came back. He asked Msgr. Dutzow and Father Mike to go with him after all. His only explanation: "My cousins could use some help."

* * *

The grand inquisitor abruptly hung up the phone. He had been talking to his comrades, members of the original terrorist cell in Stockholm, and they were not happy. Negative publicity was not what they wanted. As they viewed things, the Cardinal had to sign the confession or this whole affair would be a total failure and a profound embarrassment to The Sword of Justice. "Do whatever it takes," they told him. "But secure that confession!"

"Bring the cardinal to me," the inquisitor ordered. "We need to put an end to his stubbornness—by torture if necessary."

But before the inquisitor's order could be carried out,

there was a loud banging on the armory's front door.

"See what that's all about," the inquisitor demanded. His henchman did as he was told and slid back the slot that allowed him to see outside. Four young men each with a full head of jet-black hair stood at the door. Each was wearing a white shirt and black pants. One of the men said they had a message for the grand inquisitor.

The inquisitor responded saying, "We'll let one of you come in, but not all four. And remember, we're heavily armed. If you want to get out again alive, don't try anything foolish."

The young man who had been the spokesman stepped forward. He was frisked, and when it was clear that he had no weapons, he was allowed into the armory.

"Who are you?" the Inquisitor asked.

"My name is Dominic Turiddu. I came here today from Sicily along with my brother and two of my cousins. One of the priests you're holding hostage is a revered member of our family. We are here to demand that you to let him and his friends go. Now."

"What makes you think I'm going to do what you ask?"

"You are not a fool. You value your freedom and your life, and you know that if you refuse my request there will be consequences, serious consequences—for you and for your organization."

"You're bluffing," said the inquisitor who was not at all sure he was. "How do I know you can carry out this threat?"

"You don't know, but you're smart enough not to risk finding out the hard way. You have a choice to make, *signore*. Please make it now."

The inquisitor looked at the young man standing before him. His Sicilian eyes were fierce and uncompromising, while the rest of his demeanor was perfectly calm. Silently, the inquisitor cursed the old priest who had caused him so much trouble. He did not want to give up now—especially since his comrades in Stockholm expected him to obtain that confession—but something told him that it would be a grave mistake to make mortal enemies of the Turiddu family.

"I need to consult with my comrades," the inquisitor said. "You can either wait with your cousin or leave now. As you prefer."

"I will remain with Father Turiddu and his friends, but don't keep us waiting long. My brother and cousins are not patient men."

"I understand, *Signore* Turiddu. You'll have my answer in just a few minutes."

The terrorists took the young Sicilian to the room where his cousin, the Cardinal and Msgr. Leone were being held.

"Dom, I'm so glad you're here," Father T said to his cousin. "When are we getting out of here?"

"Very soon, Father. Your plan has been set in motion."

"What plan?" Msgr. Leone asked.

"Please be patient," Dominic replied. "Everything will be explained very soon."

* * *

Dominic Turiddu's brother and cousins were not at all patient. In fact, while he was speaking with the grand inquisitor, Father T's cousins, accompanied by the three priests from America, were crawling through the secret subterranean tunnels of Naples that date back to Greco-Roman times. The tunnels were extensive, covering the entire length and breadth of the old city. History records that they were large enough to accommodate troops of the Eastern emperor Justinian who conquered *Neapolis* (the new city) in a.d. 536 by crawling inside a water conduit leading under the city walls and attacking the Roman forces from within and without.

Now, three young Sicilians and three middle-aged Americans—all united by their love and respect for Father T—crawled through those same dark, rat-infested tunnels.

"My God, it stinks in here!" Father Mike said. "And it's hotter than hell."

"Are we sure we know where we're going?" Msgr. Dutzow asked.

"My cousins know what they're doing," said Msgr. Cugino. "We have to trust them."

When the six rescue team members reached their destination—the old armory—they quietly removed the grates and let themselves into the cellar. Father T's cousins were armed with pistols and knives, but Msgr. Cugino implored them, once again, to avoid violence if at all possible.

As it turned out, the three Sicilians surprised The Sword of Justice terrorists and quickly overwhelmed them without firing a shot or using their knives. Now it was the grand inquisitor's turn to be held hostage.

Father T was not the least bit surprised when the rest of his cousins walked through the door of the makeshift prison, but when he saw Mike and John and Vinnie, he could hardly believe his eyes.

"What took you so long?" he said with a smile. "Now, can we please get out of here!"

GLI ULTIMI GIORNI

(The Final Days.)

The Cardinal and his five priest-friends were taken back to Rome that afternoon by Interpol's chief inspector and his driver in a large black SUV. It was a quiet ride. Everyone was exhausted from the tensions of the past several days.

The Sisters welcomed the Cardinal with enthusiasm and great relief. They offered to prepare the evening meal for them, and although the priests protested that it wasn't necessary, the Cardinal insisted.

"It's the least we can do after everything you've done for me personally and for the Church we all love so much," he said.

During *cena*, which included rigatoni alla norcina and veal saltimbocca, the Cardinal once again expressed his profound gratitude to Father T and his priest-friends from his former archdiocese for their loyalty and their courage.

"No man ever had better friends, and no bishop has ever had better priests," he said. "I thank you, and so does Holy Mother Church. Without your intervention, we might have had another prolonged scandal—or at least a media circus that we certainly don't need right now."

"One question, Sal," Msgr. Cugino said. "How did our cousins from Sicily know where to find you?"

"Michael O'Keefe, the seminarian from St. Margaret of Scotland. I told him that if he didn't hear from me he should have his rector call the head of Vatican security and find out what he knew about our situation. Once Michael knew what was happening, he called Gioacchino who, in turn, called the family in Sicily. Once Dominic and the other boys arrived in Naples, they had no trouble locating us."

"But how did they know about the tunnels?" Msgr. Dutzow asked.

"I have no idea," Father T said. "But don't ever underestimate us Turiddus!"

"We never have, Sal," Father Mike responded. "And, believe me, we never will."

Father T called Marisa after supper, and she arranged an early morning flight for everyone except, of course, the Cardinal who remained at his residence off the *Via Conciliazione*. Interpol and Vatican security both said they wanted to keep a close eye on him, but they assured him it was safe to return to his work for the Apostolic Signatura.

"With all respect, it would be wise for you to refrain from making any controversial remarks, *Eminenza*, at least for a time," the chief inspector had admonished him.

"I am called to speak the truth with love, Inspector, but I promise to be judicious in my exercise of this responsibility—at least for a time."

"Thank you, *Eminenza*, we would not want to create further difficulties for your American friends."

"Indeed, we would not," said the Cardinal.

The priests mainly slept on the plane the next morning, and when they arrived back home (after going through customs and changing planes in Chicago) at around 7 p.m. local time, they were met by a delegation of family members and friends including Father T's niece Anna, Msgr. Leone's ers

sister Clare, Marisa, Jesse Lindbergh and Father T's parishioners, Joe and Rosemary Lindell.

"What in the world happened to you guys?" Anna asked. "Are you going to tell us the story or do we have to wait until it's on the front page of the paper?"

"That rag? Never!" Father T practically shouted. "We're keeping this whole business under wraps. But if you want to hear the whole story, come to the Osteria tomorrow night. We'll have dinner there and chitchat. Right now, all we want to do is go home!"

Strangely enough, the whole affair, which involved the brazen kidnapping of a prominent Cardinal and two American priests, and the wildest accusations of crimes committed by the Catholic Church throughout the ages, remained completely "under wraps" as Father T predicted it would. Not a single story appeared in the media—in Italy, in Europe or in the United States. It was as if it never happened.

That bizarre fact was one of the topics discussed intently by the large group of family members and friends who gathered in the Osteria's private dining room the following night.

"Truth is stranger than fiction," Father T said. "What we just experienced is the stuff of mystery novels. The nonsense written about the Vatican and the Church by novelists like Dan Brown fails to even come close to the truth. We just lived through an experience none of us will ever forget," Father T said. "End of conversation."

"I'll never forget the smell in the sewers of Naples," Msgr. Cugino said. "Or the sight of our three Sicilian cousins armed with knives and guns overpowering the terrorists and saving the day!"

"What did the terrorists really hope to accomplish?" Father T's niece asked.

"To embarrass the Cardinal and further their left-wing agenda by implicating the Church in one more scandal," Father T responded.

"Truth really is stranger than fiction," Msgr. Dutzow said. "We've all witnessed things—horrible things—that are an embarrassment to the Church and her clergy. But the Church remains holy even when the people who serve the Church are not."

"What's for supper?" Father T asked?

"The Norcini brothers have outdone themselves tonight," Father Mike answered. "Soup, pasta, chicken spiedini, rissoto, broccoli and your choice of dessert."

"In spite of the wonderful meal at the Cardinal's residence last night, I still feel like I haven't eaten in weeks," Msgr. Leone said. "The bread and water we were given in the Naples armory was not exactly *un pasto delizioso!*"

"There's no place quite like the Osteria—anywhere in the world!" Father Mike said. "The food is wonderful, but the people who prepare it, and the family and friends who gather to share it, make all the difference!"

Let's drink to the Cardinal!" Msgr. Cugino said. "*Cent' Anni!*

"And to the Church!" Msgr. Dutzow added.

"And to the best friends and family that ever lived!" Msgr. Leone said.

"*Il fine della storia!*" Father T added.

End of story